Will

Diamondsong

A Concerto in Ten Parts

Part 07:
Will

E.D.E. Bell

Atthis Arts
Detroit, Michigan

Diamondsong
Part 07: Will

Copyright ©2020 by E.D.E. Bell
edebell.com

This is a work of fiction.
Any resemblance to actual pyrsi, winged or otherwise, is purely coincidental.

Cover Art by M.C. Krauss

Map of Ada-ji by Ulla Thynell

Interior Design by G.C. Bell

Editorial Services by:
Catherine Jones Payne, Quill Pen Editorial
Kelsey Ronan
M. Cusack

All rights reserved.

Published by Atthis Arts, LLC
Detroit, Michigan
atthisarts.com

ISBN 978-1-945009-52-5

Library of Congress Control Number: 2019954084

First Edition: Published January 2020

This book is dedicated to Col Larry Benson

for reassuring me that the correct article for *mission* is *a*.

PREFACE

Sometimes you just have to keep pushing forward. My life has been a lot of that these past few years. Getting out of my old environment. Getting into a new one. Working through anxiety, depression, and loss. Writing this volume—through constant interruptions and setbacks. It's been beautiful, but it's been a lot.

I told you previously where I was at when I wrote this, and I hope the fact that I wrote the section focused on will, determination, perseverance—and the recognition that life involves a whole lot of detours—while I was feeling those things adds to the sense of this piece of the story. I was starting to recover, too, and the volume turns toward elements of that humor, that hope, the light emerging in the distance. Of joy.

Let me tell you about the dedication. As much as there is a canon of Emily breaking through the military culture of older men, those same men provided me strength, inspiration, and advice that has formed a great deal of who I am now. The Bible quote starting the second volume—which was made gender neutral and that was so edgy for this person—was provided on my departure by a good friend and dedicated fundamentalist Christian, who, though he knew I did not share his religion, provided me his own way of encouragement and support. That quote means so much to me, partially because he respected my authenticity while staying true to his. That is friendship.

As for Colonel Larry Benson, this is a man I think would not mind the direct mention. A hero from the Silent Generation, he gave me so much good advice over the decade I worked on the Air Force Base (if you didn't know that, yes, I have a *whole backstory*) and was such a dedicated friend. I was nervous to tell him that I was leaving what he considered a vital field of work, himself having stayed long into what would have been his retirement because, "We can't let them win." (*Them* being the bullies, the bigots, and the crooks. The ones on the inside.) Yet someone told on me, and Larry made a point of tracking me down, with finger extended. "I'm proud of you," he said. He went on to say he knew I'd make a difference wherever I was. That I would never give up. "A lot of us understand a lot more than you think we do," he said. And when he signed my going away book, he said they would miss many things about me including my "dedication to a mission" and that wording choice really moved me. Because I'd just spent almost twenty years hearing about *the* mission (often capitalized). It's a very specific phrase.

I learned so much from friends like these. How to just keep going sometimes when you have to, but *never* abandoning yourself along the way. Hey, guys—I got this.

On the subject of mentors and heroes, I want to mention the passing of my friend Alonza McKenzie in 2019. His untimely death swiped a piece out of me that I had hoped would heal, but I now realize is gone forever. Al believed in art, education, generosity, hard work, and faith. He loved Detroit. He loved music. He loved community. I will do everything I can to live up to his expectations for me, whatever the detours.

So much gratitude goes to the entire team, who all contributed to me getting through this one, which now in a new year and with new hopes, I am glad to share with you. So, to a very busy group of editors and friends: Catherine Jones Payne, Kelsey Ronan, Meghan Cusack, Camille Gooderham Campbell, Sasha Kasoff Moore, Laura Johnson, Deborah Reilly (who has continued to proofread through heart surgery recovery!), and Maria Judge—so much love and gratitude. You're all the actual best. As the kids say. Or, now, me.

Let's do this.

E.D.E. Bell

January 2020

The World of Ada-ji

The Ja-lal: A humanoid species, dwelling in the foothills and plains of Ada-ji, characterized by broad advancements in construction, invention, and health. The Fo-ror call them brutes.

The Fo-ror: A winged humanoid species, dwelling in the forests of Ada-ji, characterized by their natural living and the use of magical powers, known as valence. The Ja-lal call them fairies.

The Ja-lal and Fo-ror are similar in form, with gray skin, but differences between them in composition and culture. Pyr is singular for a Ja-lal or Fo-ror and pyrsi is plural.

The pyrsi of Ada-ji hold many **gender identities**. While this doesn't clarify all aspects of gender, it is polite to introduce oneself with a prefix, indicating the appropriate pronouns:

Fe' indicates a set of feminine identities, using the pronouns she/her/her(s).

Ma' indicates a set of masculine identities, using the pronouns he/him/his.

Ji' indicates a set of spectrum identities, using the pronouns ve/ver/vis.

When gender is unknown, it is polite to refer to a pyr with xe/xem/xyr(s). Any group of pyrsi (plural) would be referred to with they/them/their(s).

A pyr may be generically referred to as **Burge**, short for the more formal Burgess, often for purposes of polite address or getting a stranger's attention. This is similar to the use of Sir or Ma'am on Earth. For those who hold social prejudice based on class, the term implies some sense of status or honor.

Ja-lal and Fo-ror may live up to 50 cycles. Their lives are divided into defined **epochs**, aligning with societal expectations:

Aoch	Age 0-9	Characterized by upbringing, education, and exploration
Bakh	Age 10-19	Centered on building family, performing and completing apprenticeships, and finalizing life plans
Gamh	Age 20-29	Fully immersed in their specialty or role, contributing full-time to society
Dorh	Age 30-39	Respected in leadership and/or advisory roles; it is normal to take some time for self
Eroh	Age 40+	Expected to retire and engage in craft or occasional consulting, through the **life expectancy of around 50 cycles**.

Expectations differ for each culture. For example, while a Ja-lal must develop xyr profession into a career, a Fo-ror's profession and rank are set based on xyr social class and other historical and cultural factors.

A **cycle** on Ada-ji is perhaps up to four times the length of an Earth year. So, our main character, at age 20.5 cycles, has lived more than 80 Earth years but, in relation to her life span, could be considered at the **maturity of her early forties** on Earth.

Each **turn** on Ada-ji, a period of day and then night, is **significantly longer than an Earth day**. As such, pyrsi do not sleep according to light or dark, but instead based on their own needs, lifestyle, profession, and schedule.

The Ja-lal measure time by the periodic sounding of bells; they refer to the resultant time periods with the same term. The Fo-ror are less rigid about time-keeping and refer to the equivalent time period as a span. Each **bell**, or **span**, consists of more than two Earth hours.

Smaller amounts of time are referred to by both cultures as **takes**, which can be thought of as about ten Earth minutes.

In Earth terms, it has been about seven weeks since the beginning of our tale.

The Ja-lal and Fo-ror live on separate sides of the Great Cliff. They have not interacted since the ***Great War***, an event most noted for being the **end of the Violence** on Ada-ji.

Synopsis to Here

Just after Dime had left her career working for
the Circles, the government of the Ja-lal, three hooded figures burst
into her home, determined to take her away. Dime and her spouse,
Dayn, ran to escape them.

The intruders were revealed to be Fo-ror, commonly called
fairies. These fairies, unseen since the conclusion of the Great War,
were feared and loathed by the Ja-lal, who were taught that any
contact would cause the Violence to return.

Dime escaped the city and was rescued by a large animal species
known as newts, where she befriended a young newt she called
Juni. Dime was found there by a fe'pyr familiar with fairies, Ella,
who broke the news that Dime was biologically a Fo-ror—one whose
wings had been removed.

Later, Ella explained that the magical fairy power of valence
did not come from the wings, but from the heart. At her recommen-
dation, Dime traveled to the diamond caves, where she confirmed
and practiced her powers. There, she discovered that the Ja-lal also
have powers of valence, more internally directed. Dime believes
very few Ja-lal are aware of, and thus intentionally shaping, their
own powers.

Trying to make sense of these events, Dime traveled between
the lands of the fairies, the Heartland, and her own Sol's Reach. She
reconnected with friends: Zael, who she has now seen is dying, Ador,
the founder of an advocacy group called the Free Winds, Ador's
spouse Batu, and Dime's own family: Dayn, Luja, and Tum. She was
surprised to run into Rock, an Intel Agent and former flame who
had rushed to her rescue upon learning of Dime's original escape.

She encountered new allies: Volana, a fairy connected to a secret
Fo-ror discussion group, the Foundry, Volana's friend Uchitar, who

struggles with tzetz-addiction, and Hin, a young assistant Ador has taken under his charge.

Dime met with the leaders of each land. First, High Seat Ferala, who confessed that Dime was part of an old scheme to avenge the horrors of a disease called the curse, which the Fo-ror blamed on the Ja-lal. This scheme, designed by now Third Seat Neimano, was named Project Diamondsong. His plan was to remove the wings from Fo-ror newborns, place them in positions of potential influence amongst the Ja-lal, and then allow them to grow up before activating their loyalties as Fo-ror spies. Later, she met with Sala, the Light, who was resistant to her message of working with the Fo-ror.

Dime was able to locate three other potential victims of Neimano: Kolk, Nafat, and Olok. Olok, a respected medic, conveyed her belief that Jaza, leader of the Sol's Pillars, is likely one as well.

Dime secretly observed a gathering led by High Seat Ferala and Second Seat Layanie. Afterward, Dime was stopped by an officer of a political group, the Risers, named Intinpalo. Dime and Rock got into an argument, and Rock left abruptly. Frustrated by this and Intinpalo's supremacist language, Dime showed him the net that held the newts back from their natural home as evidence of Fo-ror flaws.

After he left, Dime was unexpectedly joined in the forest by her children, along with two of the newts: Juni and Stern Eyes. Then, Neimano and one of his guards found them, attacking her and the others with valence. Stern Eyes reacted in fear, using her own valence to stop Neimano and his guard.

Feeling the urgency of bringing more voices to their cause, Dime and her family traveled to a place known as the Underground, where Fo-ror and Ja-lal live together in secret. She tried to spread what she knew about the changing mood of Ada-ji and the real threat of war, but her talks were met with mixed reactions. She is still shaken from the harsh words thrown at her by a stranger there.

Yet, word is spreading of the coalition for peace. Dime is back in her city of Lodon, ready to work with her allies to gather momentum.

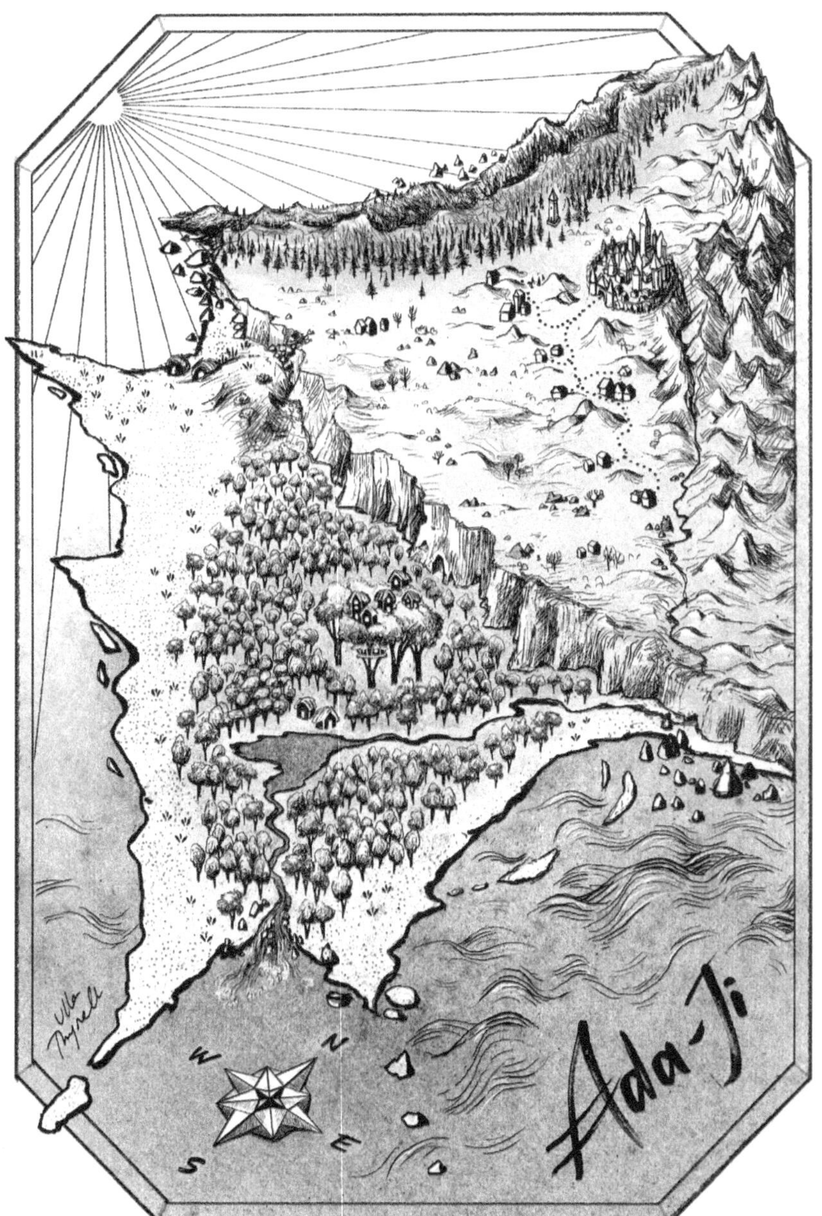

Ada-Ji
W
N
E
S

Will

All my forty-three years I have been a good soldier. The time is growing late, and I can't be a good soldier any longer.

—Shirley Chisholm, 1968

Аct 1

Plans

Pats of cloved butter dissolved into the fresh stack of flatcakes as Batu poured a dark brew from the stained kettle. Over each steaming mug, she tipped in a measure of castanut cream from a small ceramic pitcher. "There," she said, sitting down next to Dime at the long, oval table.

Batu had insisted on another meal before Dime left to start meeting with some of the Free Winds participants in the city. Any impatience she'd felt over her friend's coddling had disappeared as the batter hit the pan. Far from achieving perfection in her ethics, Dime could absolutely be swayed by food.

"Do you need anything?" Batu asked.

Dime held back a snort. *Seconds?* Instead, she scooped her utensil into the soft cakes, watching them compress and then release as she pulled the bite toward her. "No, this is perfect. Do you make the butter yourself?"

"I do," Batu answered, in between sips of the brew. "I grow the cloves on the deck in batches. When they're ready to harvest, I mince them in with a three-oil blend, stir in some smashed black pepper and a sprinkling of salt, then let them set into a mold. Usually by the time we're out, the next batch is ready."

Dime shook her head. The flavor was exceptional.

For a while, Dime had assumed the bright yellow drape Batu was wearing was a cooking apron. She'd almost commented on how nice it was, but then hesitated, as Batu seemed to keep it on regardless of her activity. Then, she realized, she could compliment it either way. "Batu, that yellow is a pretty color on you."

Bringing forward the ruffled rose fabric on her sleeves, Batu ran her hands down the yellow outer garment, her smile broadening. "Oh, thank you. I like to wear it during the nighttime, to remind me of Sol. I love nighttime," she clarified, "but I've always been more of a daylight pyr."

Dime wondered whether Batu had spent time outside of the city, where the nights were as dark as the glow from the skystones let them be. Here upcity, not far from where Dime used to live, the night was glitter—rows of tower windows twinkled outside, illuminating a maze of sky alleys and outdoor pavilions. Batu had mentioned visiting the Heartland someturn. Only there were the nights truly dark, in the layered cover of the thick trees. Except for in the city, where glowstones hung in every direction, softer, but no less bright than the lamps of Lodon.

She remembered the little gardens growing around the base of the trees in the neighborhoods of Pito, often with a long bench and a border of flowers. Dime could hardly imagine what Batu could do with one of those, given what she'd been able to craft from just deckside planters.

Not to say Batu's home was small. This was the largest kitchen table she'd ever seen, despite only two pyrsi living here. Their main room, which opened to the generous stone deck, was sectioned into a foyer, a table area, and then a gathering of fine seats. Two sleeping rooms had private wash spaces, and beyond them was a separate library and office. Circling around much of the tower's side, the space was designed such that all the main rooms had wide windows looking out on the city.

Dime continued to gaze out at the city lights as she finished every last bite of the meal. "Batu, you mustn't tell Dayn, but your flatcakes are strictly the best."

Batu grinned. Ador and Dayn had been best friends for so long, there was no doubt Dayn already knew.

"I'm ready to go, after this," Dime said. "Fears and posters and all."

Her expression growing serious, Batu nodded. To Dime's relief, the fe'pyr had taken the news of Dime's origin without so much as a blink. Though Dime couldn't attest to what she'd thought inside, she hadn't made any deal of it, something Dime had appreciated a lot.

Yet Batu knew, as Dime did, that flyers throughout the city declared Dime's fairy origins and that she'd used those powers to commit the Violence. There was no way for her to interact anymore without invoking strong reactions. Fear, disgust, outrage—or worse.

Admittedly, her now full crop of white hair wouldn't help, but Dime liked it and so she was keeping it. If nothing else, it felt like the one thing she could choose for herself lately. Or maybe the Underground had influenced her a touch. There, her hair really hadn't been of note, and that feeling—the feeling of nothing—had been one she could get used to. Part of her had wanted to stay. A greater part had known she couldn't. Off she'd gone. Again.

After leaving the hidden city, Dime had arrived here without much incident. She'd become used to flying around the buildings while avoiding being seen, partly because in a city without flying beings, pyrsi weren't used to looking up. Yet there were still plenty of windows, so Dime used the tower walls and sky alleys to her advantage, keeping to solid sections and zig-zagging so she didn't stray into anyone's view for long. The precision of her valence much improved, she'd set the chair down right on Batu's outdoor deck. Which, now that she thought about it, did smell strongly of clovebulbs.

She'd returned here at Ador's insistence, for Ador and Batu had a fully-furnished guest suite. Dime knew her presence would be discovered in time; she'd worried about putting their home at risk.

Batu had silenced that immediately. "You've provided pyrsi the catalyst to finally spread open discussion regarding the fairies. You think I'm going to stay here, hiding, when we can help?" Batu hadn't wanted to hear a word elsewise.

Yet Batu didn't know the change that had occurred in Dime over her stay at the Underground. She knew there'd been some trouble at one of the talks, and sure, it'd been a small thing, but the doubt that one exchange had planted continued to sap her energy like a hot coal sitting on snow. In words she wouldn't speak aloud, she almost wanted to stay here, not think about anything that had happened, and let other pyrsi deal with it. Pyrsi with thicker skin. Or no emotions. Or an unquestionable past. Or whatever it was.

That wasn't right either; Dime did want to help. But she also didn't want to be scared of every action, of every bell spent awake, not having anywhere she could feel safe.

It had taken her a great deal to work up to talking to Batu about it. The two fe'pyrsi hadn't really been close, not like Dime was with Ador. But she couldn't let the uncertainty wear her down further than it already had, so she'd finally told Batu she needed to talk.

"I'm just so scared, now, to be in the open. And it's not like I don't think I should be told if I'm wrong; we all learn so much from each other. You know that." She'd glanced in mild desperation at Batu, just hoping she'd understand. "But never knowing when someone is going to attack me over some unnuanced ideal—without even knowing me—I don't know. I feel ridiculous. Even talking about it feels selfish." She'd glanced away.

Batu had paused. "I wish I could tell you to ignore them." She sat back in the chair. "But I've seen it myself, with the Winds. One unkind voice drowns a thousand calls for reason. And if you're affected, as you've been, we need to help you heal." The clicking of her fingernails against the wood let Dime know Batu was still thinking.

"I have an idea," she finally said. "Ador is used to speaking. He deals better with the reactions. Your piece is helpful too, but we'll measure it out. Smaller groups. Pyrsi we know, at least for now. We'll give pyrsi the opportunity to hear your story and perspectives, but the organization will be the outward face." Batu looked up. "What do you think?"

Dime hadn't known what to think. Honestly, it felt like she was backing out, or that she wasn't strong enough, or that she was as awful as they'd said. After all, lots of pyrsi were being affected; her own issues didn't compare to that. "There's just so much urgency," she'd muttered, not wanting to burden Batu with the rest of it.

"Everyone contributes in their own way," Batu had said. "You wearing out does no one any good. Trust. Trust in all of us, working together. Ador is good at what he does. He endures it. Dime, you be Dime."

She wasn't sure. But she could at least trust her for a while, until she got her head put on right. "Where do you recommend I go first?"

"I have ideas on that, but I was hoping we could talk about the message. Telling your story is a start, but we'll want to offer concrete ways to help as well."

Dime thought about this. She remembered the conversations she'd had at the Underground, but also considered that Lodon culture was different. It was that difference, really, that prompted her in this direction. "I think we should mostly start encouraging pyrsi to talk openly about the Fo-ror. They won't be used to doing so, but eventually it will grow familiar. The Circles can't hush something we're all discussing." Batu had nodded. "We can let them know where to go to talk about it, to learn more about the fairies or to participate with us. How to contact the Free Winds." Feeling that was oversimplified but not knowing what to add, she'd sat and waited for a reply.

Batu had pressed the rounded back of a tea spoon against her lips. "Smaller ways also. Pyrsi have lives, they have important things to do. We can't stop the wheels from turning while we push the cart. Or sometimes it's just a lot for a pyr." Dime understood that. "So we need to give them ways they can help within their communities, within their own lives. What?" she'd added, noting Dime's pained expression.

"All of this will take time to develop. Time we may not have."

"The world is complicated," Batu had replied without a pause. "Better to understand that than to turn, ourselves, to control as the solution."

Batu had seemed so certain. Dime wished she could be certain again. At least, she'd felt better as they'd continued to plan, discussing their approaches, including where and whom in the city she could visit.

And, now, stuffed with flatcakes, she was ready to get to it. She hoped.

Batu had moved over to the basin and was rinsing out the mugs.

Dime watched the flickering lights through the window, trying to prepare herself for being out in the city again. As much as Batu insisted she was still just Dime, it wasn't fair to say things hadn't changed. Pyrsi now believed Dime was a fairy, at least as they'd see it. That news, much more concerning than their original view of her as a Ja-lal victim of the fairies, would change their reactions to her presence; it simply had to. She pulled her gaze away. "How many of the Free Winds would you say are comfortable with the idea of fairies?" she asked, winding a napkin in her fingers.

Batu set the mugs down onto a towel and grabbed another one to dry off the table. She tossed the cloth deftly into a bin and sat down next to Dime. "Oh, that's hard to answer. In the Winds, when we've discussed the fairies, we've started with the fact that they are real. So our discussions always went past what most of the population would endure, those pretending they aren't.

"Still, mixed views. There are some, like Ador, who've never believed the fairies were any specific danger, no more than any group of pyrsi. As you know, Ador visited them, in the shared areas, and confirmed this for himself." Dime knew Batu was referring to the Crossing and the Underground, the two areas in between the two lands where fairies and solies met, worked, and even lived together.

"As for comfortable," she continued. "What is comfortable? Willing to meet a fairy? Hug one? Willing to hold a biscuit with one?

Willing to engage in business together? Entrust them with your children? Watch your child marry one?" She looked up, a sharpness in her eyes. "Willing to share governance of Ada-ji? Willing to live under the rule of one? You see, there are all levels of comfortable.

"The majority of the Free Winds *believe* they are comfortable, and so that's the right first step. And there are others who *say* they are comfortable, but harbor thoughts to the contrary. Then there are still some openly against it." She grimaced. "That's the trick of a free-thought society, right? Not everyone will think the same. However, as long as they are not overtly harmful, we allow participants to stay. There are always limits, but that's our general view. Better for them to stay and be part of the dialogue than to be pushed away to satisfy someone's else's sense of righteousness."

The way she said that last bit, Dime got the impression there had been heated debates on that very subject. She hesitated to ask the next part. "What about Hin? He's been uncomfortable with the fairies."

"I know." She paused. "He'll come around."

But Batu hadn't seen him at the den, or later at the Underground. "He hid in his suite almost the whole time we were there." She'd promised not to mention the secret city, but Batu would know. "Ador was so busy talking to pyrsi, I don't think he took it seriously enough. I talked to Hin for a little while when he stopped by, though I think he only left his room because he heard Luja was there. It's . . . frustrating, when he has direct access to Ador, and he's met so many fairies now."

Batu's expression changed slowly, as if she was considering how to respond. "Pyrsi won't all adjust immediately," she finally said. "If you reject them when they don't, rather than openly reject their prejudice, you restrict their room to change. There are different views, but that is mine." She shifted in her seat.

"I'm not excusing it," she continued. "It upsets me too! But it's important to understand the strength of the messages some of us received. Your father is such a loving, open ma'pyr. You probably didn't hear as much from him, or in the places he would have associated. Some of us were raised in homes that mentioned the fairies in casual use. As warnings. As metaphors. Even as curses. I know I didn't think about it turn-to-turn, but I internalized it over cycles. It took me a while, of meeting pyrsi who steered me otherwise, who sometimes shocked me with blunt insight and uncomfortable stories, to accept that all those hints and whispers were promoting an idea that not only wasn't true, but was harmful. I wouldn't be here today, doing this, if they had pushed me out on my early reactions. I try to remember that."

Dime would never have thought Batu was once prejudiced about fairies, as openly as she embraced them now. She wondered if Batu was embarrassed, despite her matter-of-fact recounting. Though, maybe this was the message she was delivering to Hin; to recognize how he felt and then move past it. Dime was going to have to understand these different reactions now, not just being out there talking, but having pyrsi see her as a fairy, herself. As they would, thanks to those flyers.

Her sigh was a bit loud.

"Hey, it's not all bad," Batu offered. "Some are quite positive these turns." She glanced away.

That sounded weird. Dime peered at her suspiciously. Ador and Batu always got the same inflection when they were holding something back. She and Dayn had often chuckled about it.

"Please, you have to tell me now. I know there's something." Her chest pinched. That was the thing lately; every new conversation made her anxious for what would come of it. She wished she could just return to living and being happy, without always worrying what barbs she might grasp. She supposed that's what everyone wanted. It was just whether they wanted it for themselves, or for everyone else, too.

"The Fairy Fanatics."

Dime stared at her friend.

"It's a new club. Run by a museum curator. Took a fancy to the idea of fairies since they were in town, you know, and he's started a club about it. They meet just to talk about how great the fairies are. Lavish parties. Art. He's commissioned a whole set of murals."

She would have snorted if she wasn't so glued to the wall over this. Fairy Fanatics? Museum curator? *Murals?* "Ma'Nafat?" she offered.

"Yes, that sounds right. Do you . . ." Batu's eyes narrowed. "Do you know him?"

"We've met," she answered with enough of a tone that Batu wasn't going to press. "But fancy—yes, that's him." She shook her head, a host of concerns forming. "Well, there's that. Do you have the map?" Batu had been going to show her the Free Winds' gathering places, and she was ready to be distracted.

"Sure," Batu said, pulling a map of the city from a cabinet and spreading it over the long table. "So, this is the old-crew meeting place we've discussed." She pointed. "I still recommend you start there. They vary their meeting schedule, but someone is usually around so you can at least set something up. It's a solid, tight-knit group; they won't react too strongly to your presence, and they may have good ideas about next steps."

Her chest pinched again. No, she reminded herself, these were allies. It hurt Dime immeasurably that she was now scared of allies, too. She tried to remember Batu's advice.

A light tap sounded at the door. Batu beamed. "Come in," she called, moving out into the living area to greet her spouse. Dime rose behind her, knowing there was no need to conceal the map or hide herself from view. If there were a concern, Ador wouldn't offer his friendly rap. Dime followed out through the archway.

With the door now open, Ador reached over to encircle Batu in a warm embrace as Hin squeezed in behind him. "Oh, and I just cleaned up!" Batu said, moving over to embrace the much taller Hin. "No matter; are you hungry?" She ushered Hin back into the kitchen area, where Dime could hear her pouring another mug of brew. Ador stretched, then smiled at Dime.

"How was the drive?" Dime asked.

"My joints resent me," he answered.

Whatever Dime was going to respond, she was quickly distracted by the guilty look on Ador's face. "What?" she asked. "Is this the Fairy Fanatics?"

"Pardon?" By his blank response, he had not heard about Nafat's fan club.

"Just, what is it?" She knew she shouldn't be so blunt, but she just couldn't take secrets anymore, not with the fear inside that wouldn't leave, and especially not knowing she was about to face a city full of gasping reactions, rude remarks, and overly polite greetings. And even her friends kept making tight faces, like they knew things she didn't.

He lowered his voice. "Dayn is completely absorbed in studying the rock structure."

This was no surprise. Dayn took his career seriously and would welcome any chances for new research. So that wasn't it. Dime raised her brows.

Ador sighed. "Oh, I don't even want to tell you. So. Tum couldn't stop fretting about the newts, and Luja backed her up. They wore him down, Dime. Besides, Luja really is grown. And you know ve'd never do anything to put vis little sibling at risk."

Dime squinted. "What are you saying? They went to the Beds?" When Ador didn't answer, she sucked in a breath. "But it's on the other side of Ada-ji! They can't be by themselves, they—"

"They got a lift. From fairies. They do this all the time, carrying pyrsi around on special tarps. They were pyrsi we trusted, Dime. They left through the Heartland entrance, the lower one, and didn't use valence until they were downshore. They took them all the way there, made sure they were safe, then came back. I didn't leave until they returned."

Was he really saying her children had gallivanted off to the Heartland *by themselves*? And he and Dayn had let them? She wasn't sure whether to fall into her worry or her shock. "Does Tum have her chair?" she rasped out instead.

Ador shook his head. "She didn't want it. Says it's too sandy there, and Juni carries her just fine." He grimaced. "Dayn did have some trouble with that, but Tum told him to trust her; it's her chair. I have it with me, in my car. Look, I was surprised he let them go, after . . . what happened."

That's right; Ador knew that the newts had used valence. That they even had it. That was a secret they'd agreed to keep as tight as possible for now. Not even Volana knew.

They stopped as Hin walked out into the living room with Batu. "No, really, it's fine," Hin was saying. "I just want to get back to my own space for a while. I have plenty to eat there."

"Alright. We'll see you at the dome, then?"

"I'll come back here first, to see if you're here. But, yes." Hin gave Batu a light hug, before turning to Dime. "See you soon," he said. Dime nodded back, and Hin stepped out of the door. She'd wanted to talk to him sooner rather than later, but she was still spinning with the news about her children. So she watched as the door swung shut.

"We found him a room just a few floors down," Ador said, staring at the closed door. He turned to Batu. "Luja and Tum went to stay with the newts. Alone. I was just breaking the news to their mother."

Batu grimaced.

"Look, I know," Ador said to them both. "He felt reasonably sure they'd be fine. He said that the newts treat them as cubs; they won't view them as outsiders. He thought maybe them being there might help, in case— Well, honestly, I don't know. He agreed to it." Ador raised his hands to his sides.

Reasonably sure? "What about their school?" Dime blurted. "Luja was learning from the medics, and we had Tum in classes there."

"I don't know," Batu offered, her voice tentative. "Living within another culture sounds like a unique education to me."

But school wasn't the issue. It was the other thought. "What if the Fo-ror go there? Or worse?" She knew that the words on her tongue would reveal information that Batu didn't know, but it wasn't fair to ask Ador to keep this from her anyway. So she said it. "What if they realize who it was who attacked Neimano, in the forest? That it wasn't me?"

She swung around to Batu. "We want to keep this as close as possible, but the newts have valence. And they used it on a fairy that attacked us."

"Oh, my," Batu said, moving over to a padded chair, where she sat, her eyes wide.

"Luja and Tum were there," Ador said, breaking the brief silence. "They know. It was a risk they were willing to take. I know they're young, and I'd be concerned too. What am I saying—I *am* concerned. But they understand. They do. Maybe we just need to . . . trust Dayn."

After a long moment, standing in between the two spouses, Dime let a huge, exasperated sigh. She'd reached her limit. "I'm sure you want to catch up. I'm fine. Just going back to the room for a bit."

Batu was still collapsed into the seat as Dime walked back into the guest room and shut the door. Rummaging in her bag, for at this point she'd given up on ever legitimately unpacking, she pulled out Rock's carved owl and thunked it down on the bedside table. She hopped up onto the bed, crossing her legs, and pivoted the owl to face her.

"Hi," she said. The owl didn't respond. "Any ideas?"

While Dime had harbored momentary hope that this was the part of her story where the owl sprung to life and started offering humorous wisdom, it just stayed there, peering back. "That's ok," she said. "See, that's my problem, too." She sort of hoped the owl would understand. Everyone told her to be who she was, but—

Anyway. "So my kids are off on their own," she said. The owl didn't answer.

Maybe there was nothing to say. Or maybe Dime had to figure it out herself. After all, this was just one more thing on her mind now: her children, alone on the beaches, without Dime knowing what had happened with the newts since Stern Eyes used her valence. Without knowing if Neimano had figured out who'd really harmed him. Dayn, still at the Underground. Zael, close to death. Nafat, running a *fan club*. And, then, on top of that, Jaza—the instigator behind all of Sol's Pillars divisive ideology—a Project Diamondsong victim herself. For Dime believed Olok's theory. She believed Olok.

Dime had finally met the Sol's Pillars leader, if briefly. Though she didn't prefer to think in such terms, she didn't like her. Jaza exuded bitterness and anger. She felt small, to Dime. Functional leaders, like Sala, frustrated her in different ways, but they at least had a larger sense of the world. Jaza was more like a bully with a real big posse.

The bells rang out over the city, echoing through the towers. Dime scooted back against the headboard and closed her eyes. She'd thought a lot about Jaza since returning to Lodon. The stress of not knowing what to do about her only added to all the other stress and fear. Only one option felt right, yet she doubted herself. She doubted everything.

Dime could reveal Jaza's secret to the city's population. It was so outlandish, they'd probably believe her. Jaza would be run out by the Pillars, the way they'd done to Dime. Without her fervent leadership and burning speeches, perhaps Sol's Pillars would wither away.

Using fear to fight fear—she wouldn't do it.

The conclusion she'd drawn: she was not going to confront Jaza at all. Not on this. Dime would confront her ideas, her approach, whatever she needed to. But she would not revictimize a pyr who was undoubtedly affected by this knowledge.

For, Dime suspected, Jaza knew.

Hard to say what did it—a friend in youth seeing her scars, an accident with valence, harsh words from someone close to her, or from a stranger. If Jaza thought the fairies were dangerous, she had reason to. Dime would not negate her experience, nor would she inspire further harm. That was the fallacy of harm in the first place—equating the action of some to the action of many to foster prejudice and division. Dime wouldn't do it.

Jaza's voice was loud, but it was small. Dime would not spend her time addressing the fe'pyr, focusing the issue on one pyr when the issue was society's to grasp. As for Ador and Volana and their coalition—their voices would be bigger.

Reopening her eyes, she blinked back at the owl. "Ok, I agree."

Ador was running his finger over the map when Dime returned to the front room.

"I was just going out to meet with the Free Winds," she said. "Batu and I have been strategizing. I knew you were coming back here, but I wasn't sure how long it would be, so I decided to get to work. I'd say we could go together now, but I do stand out these turns." She pointed at her hair.

"I've told you, it's lovely," he replied, before his expression turned serious. "We're all going to have to be in the open soon," he said. "Maybe we should have just done this before."

"Things were different before." They'd gone over this.

Uncharacteristically, Ador only shrugged.

Breaking the uncomfortable silence, she continued on. "So, the main thing is just getting around the city and talking to pyrsi. I'm going to be a lightning rod doing that, but at least I can get away now. And my children aren't around." Her chest pinched—she'd decided to stay in the city so she couldn't focus on that now. "Worst case, I can get away."

That didn't feel right, though. She wasn't trying to escape and run and hide and all those things she'd sworn she wouldn't do anymore. Nothing felt right anymore, really.

Ador seemed to read her thoughts. "That's part of why we're doing this. It won't be just you. As we build support, we won't need to put you in front of it. No one should always have to be in front of it. We'll share that." So, she realized, Batu had talked to him about their conversations here. No, that was reasonable. It was kind.

Gratitude again surged for her friends. Not just for their kindness, but for knowing that they meant it—that she would not be left alone. So she took another breath, trying to shake her feelings away. "Like we talked about back there, I was planning on organizing groups to travel to villages, first those nearby, and then farther out. To let them know the change we're looking to bring, to see who will support. To ask if they will join us in doing what they can to steady reactions and prevent the Violence as we discuss how to move forward."

"Again, you'll have more support than you may think," Ador responded. "So many will open their eyes to find themselves on the cusp. There will be resistance." He gazed off at the wall.

The unspoken rest of that thought was the part they hadn't resolved. If others resorted to the Violence before they could prevent it, what would they do? Their positive words would ring hollow in the face of force. She found no resolution, no easy answer. There was no way to plan for a score of different scenarios. Dime only knew that keeping peace must stay at the forefront of their goals as they pushed their proposals out.

"So, this is where I was going first." She pointed at the map, toward a juncture to the wesside, in an area beyond the business districts. "Batu explained their history to me. I'll swing by first, then maybe join them for one of their meetings. See what they think."

"I agree. Solid lot, there. I'd keep some of them in the city, to help us spread the message here, and then send out one team, I suppose, to the outgate villages. They'll probably propose the same thing."

"That's what I was thinking. Whelp." She rose from her seat. "Time to begin. Hey." She'd been thinking about something since Ador returned, really before Ador returned, and with those flyers around town she didn't want to delay further. "How did Hin take the news? Of my background. Just, all of it." He'd seemed happy to see Dime when he'd returned, but she wanted to know what she was dealing with before discussing the flyers.

Ador paused, holding his mouth open. "He didn't really mention it."

Dime knew what Ador was thinking, and their eyes met for an awkwardly long moment. "He heard, right? Everyone there heard."

"He was in his room a lot," Ador said. "And, yeah. He didn't bring it up." He took a breath. "Do you want me to talk to him?"

He must've heard. No one stayed that isolated. "Actually, I was going to talk to him before I left. I'd give him more time to rest after getting back, except with those flyers around town . . ." Dime paused. "I'd prefer to go to him now, provided he's not asleep. Before he sees. Can you show me where he is?"

"Certainly. Could I . . . go with you?" Ador folded the map and set it to the side.

"That might be best," she agreed. Hin viewed Ador as a mentor, and she hoped that would soften any discomfort in the conversation. She should have made an effort to talk to him at the Underground. But she'd do it now, and make sure they were fine. Besides, since he'd stayed mostly away from their group, he might have heard a different side of conversations there. She was curious what he thought. What he'd heard.

Ador headed for the door, Dime following. As he'd said, the apartment was not far, just a short walk down the stairs. The privacy turner wasn't flipped, so she went ahead and knocked.

Hin seemed surprised to see them, but he welcomed them both in. All the homes in this tower were high-end, though the way the much smaller space was awkwardly positioned behind the stairwell, Dime could see how Ador had been able to secure it for the younger pyr.

Despite the fine trimmings, it was virtually undecorated. Stacks of paper rested on the otherwise empty shelves. A single lamp sat on the table. It was set too brightly, and the light flickered over the stark walls. Not wanting to be rude, Dime tried not to glance around as she accepted the chair that Hin pulled over.

She'd normally ask how he was, but it seemed misleading given her underlying concern. So she jumped in.

"There's something I want you to know before you see it. But first, if it's ok to talk, I wanted to ask how you felt about what you learned about me . . . where we were before."

Hin grimaced. He looked at Ador.

"Hin?" Dime prompted. "I know that, well, look, I didn't know anything about fairies either, but—"

He snapped around to face Dime. "Again? I thought we talked about this. I don't see why you'd go along with making the fairies part of this when the Circles are the issue. That place . . . it felt like a trap. I was hoping you'd felt it too. After what you said."

That wasn't right. Unease gripping her gut, Dime started to wonder if Ador had been right. But surely he'd heard. "You heard . . . about me? Specifically?"

He squinted. "Maybe you need to explain?"

This was uncomfortable. "About my origins."

From his held expression, she suddenly understood. He really didn't know. *Harm.* Ador shifted in the chair beside her, but didn't speak.

"I'm sorry. I thought you'd heard. I was born in the Heartland," she said, trying to sound calm. "I didn't know this myself, but my biology is . . . Fo-ror."

Hin jumped up from his seat. "You're a *fairy?* And you didn't tell me?" Hin almost hissed the words. Dime tried to understand. She tried to think how it would feel to be the last to know.

"I'm Dime," she said, also standing. "The same Dime I've been. I really thought that you'd heard. But either way, I wanted to talk to you about it."

He stood, tense, and she couldn't read whether he was angry, hurt, or just stunned. She kept going. "There's more. There's a flyer posted around town about me. I wanted to talk to you before you saw it." He stayed still. "It says that I have valence. And it says that I committed the Violence using it."

"So that's true too?"

"No." She hesitated. "No. Only the first part. I do have valence." She removed a tin of lip balm from her pocket and spun it in the air before tucking it back into the fabric of her tunic. "The rest is misleading. Yes, I've committed the Violence, but not on purpose. Their saying it so starkly and without context misstates the truth."

He plunked down in his chair, so she sat again, vaguely aware that Ador was still beside her.

"Hin, I'm sorry to load so much at once, but I think it's time to move past these feelings about the fairies. We need your help. If we really want freedom, we need to start talking as the whole of Ada-ji, just as you've talked about the whole of Sol's Reach. Ador and I are going to ask the Free Winds to speak more openly, and Volana is talking to the Foundry right now. I know you're not fully comfortable with the Fo-ror, or fairy valence, but we'll show you. We'll show you it's all fine; they're just pyrsi. And we all need you with us to prevent the Violence from returning. Can we count on you?"

Hin stared at the wall. "I need you to leave," he said, his voice cold.

Dime's heart thumped louder and a hollowness rushed in her throat. "I'll leave if that's what you ask," she said, her breath thin. "But can we talk? See what it really is that's bothering you?"

"I don't know." He shook his head. "Just for now, can I be alone?"

"Sure," she said, trying not to overreact until she could think more about all of this. "I'll check back. We can . . . talk. Ador, let's go." Dime practically had to lead Ador out into the hallway, noting the shock on her friend's face. The door pushed closed behind them and Dime ushered him back, out of the hall and into the larger stairwell.

"I'm sorry," Ador said, spinning toward her. "I'm so sorry." He swiped at the air before crossing his arms. "As much time as I've spent with him—I took him to the Und—, and for him to—"

"It's ok." It wasn't, but this wasn't Ador's fault. "We let him be the last to know. We should have looked out more. How would you feel, learning your friend was different than you thought, and everyone else knew?"

"Dime, that's crap and you know it. It's bigotry, plain and simple. How dare he treat you like that!"

Didn't Ador know? "You think he's the first to treat me like that? Outside the gates. In the city. Even in the 'perfect' other place. They see what they want to. Labels, first. Me, never. This is what we're going to fix, Ador. We have to stay with it." Feeling close to crumbling herself, she wasn't sure where she was drawing the words from. Because Ador was right. Pyrsi were being *awful*, and her understanding was wearing thin.

Ador took a moment to calm, turning toward a tall window in the stairwell, not unlike the one Neimano had used to first find her at her own tower, just a short distance from here.

"He always does this," Ador finally said, still facing out of the window. "He reacts first, thinks second. He's young. Maybe ... maybe we need to let him think. Maybe this is what he needed; some pyrsi are like that, sadly. I mean, he was going to see it. I wouldn't have lied." He rubbed his forehead. "I'll get with him soon and find out where he stands. But this is his last chance for me. I'm not going to keep— Sol's sleepcap."

Dime raised her eyebrows.

"There's a fairy outside." Perhaps remembering her earlier ordeal, he whipped around. "It's ok. It's Volana."

She could barely keep up as the empty space inside her rushed with anticipation.

Indeed, as she edged over to her friend's side, she saw the silhouette of Volana's ribbons whipping in the wind between the glimmering towers, as Volana tried desperately to straighten a piece of paper while her wings flapped unsteadily. This high up, downcity, she would have been likely out of view, but here, anyone in the surrounding tall towers would be able to see her. Dime was glad it was dark, at least.

"Here, does this open?" Ador muttered, wrenching at the old rusted hinge. "I gave her directions to reach Batu, but there was no reason for her to be here so soon. I hope she's ok."

"Step back," Dime asked, and when he did, she sensed the window frame with her valence, reaching in to feel the curved edge of the metal hook. Shaking the roughness loose, she swung the window open. Ador started to take off his jacket, probably to wave it like a banner, and she gestured him back. "No, I've got it."

Pulling a spare tissue from her pocket, she zipped it out into the sky, flying it right in front of Volana's face and wiggling it, like a signal. Volana stopped, folding the paper back into a pocket. Dime drew the cloth back, Volana following until she eased back through the window and Dime shut it behind her.

"This way," Dime whispered without a greeting, suddenly glad Hin's oddly shaped suite did not have a window on the stairwell side, and glad as well for the distraction. Hin's words had hurt, but what they had touched was a scar, and she would not let herself sink again. Their friend was here, and that was more important.

As they hurried up the stairs, she wondered why Volana was here so soon. And even so, what sort of directions Ador could have given to guide her right to them.

Only when they were back through Ador's door did they each greet her. "Hello!" Volana answered. She reached into a long pocket and started to pull out what Dime realized were tree shoes.

"Oh, you're welcome to wear them if you're more comfortable, but there's no need. We wear our boots inside," Dime said, trying to steady her voice.

Volana's lips tightened for a flash, but she folded the tree shoes back into a pocket. Arching her back a bit, she gazed around her. "This home is beautiful," she said.

Walking in from the kitchen area, Batu gasped. "Thank you," the fe'pyr said without missing another beat. "Hello. I'm Fe'Batu."

"Yes, Ador's spouse. He speaks of you like a lone skystone guiding a deep forest path." She smiled widely.

Dime hoped Batu would realize the fairies were actually this poetic and there was no sarcasm intended, but then the fe'pyr was covered in ribbons and carried a second set of shoes. Batu didn't seem to need Dime's help.

"Yes, I'm fond of him too." Batu winked.

They paused. Dime almost introduced Volana, but wanted to make sure Volana had a chance to first. She needn't have worried.

"I am Fe'Volana, a cleaner of the city of Pito. Your city is something I could never have imagined."

Dime had first seen the structures of Pito with fresh eyes, looking upward to discover a marvel of design and nature. She tried to picture what Lodon might look like that way.

"Everything here is ... exposed." Volana paused, but seeing the others' interest, she went on. "The homes rise in the air, in an ever-torrent of wind. The mountains rise behind, as if watching. I can hardly consider what daylight feels like here, without any shelter from Sol."

Unlike the plains, the city was nothing but shelter from Sol, but Dime supposed Volana meant the towers themselves, rising like the skeletons of massive trees, but with no canopy or layers of green leaves. Through the perspective of someone who spent xyr life in the forest, a whole different city formed in her view.

"The five-fork tower was easy to find. From there, I only hoped I'd gone the right way. I was starting to worry."

Ah, so that's how she'd found them so easily. Dime had passed that cluster so many times, she hadn't considered how it would stand out as a landmark. She appreciated Ador's finesse. Oh, who was she kidding? She always appreciated Ador's finesse.

"Please, would you sit?" Batu pointed to the back corner, lined in cushioned seats and a sectioned sofa. "If you'd prefer a different chair, please let me know."

Dime couldn't help but notice how Batu's eyes glowed at having the fairy in their home. Meaning Batu still saw Dime as just herself. That felt mostly right.

"This is perfect," Volana said, perching on a corner seat.

As Batu brought a tray with water, a silence fell over the quartet. Volana would not have traveled here lightly, not so soon, when they'd already put together a plan. Something must have happened. Trying to ignore the pinch of her growing anxiety, already exacerbated by Hin's harsh reactions, Dime waited. She sipped the glass of water Batu slid into her hand.

In the lamplight of the center table, Volana's face was drawn.

"I have two pieces of news, and neither of them are good. I know I was supposed to start coordinating, but I went to check on Uchitar because it worried me that we'd been apart. And knowing where he'd gone." Her eyes flicked away. "He was arrested. He was using."

Dime turned to see whether Batu knew about the concept of arrest or of Uchitar's addiction. By her sympathetic expression, it appeared that she did. Or, she surmised it. Dime could only imagine on how many levels this pained Volana, who had worked so hard to free the ma'pyr from the deadly tzetz.

"This is part of our custom, and part of Seats' edict," Volana went on. "I would have thought, before, there is nothing to do. But meeting you, all of you,"—she waved around the table—"has made me think our decisions are our own. Uchitar, he is agonized when they take him this way. It is a prison for his prison. Being away from the tzetz would not help him, even if true. He needs more support than just no access.

"Being away like that, especially with . . . what happened to him recently . . . would only make his issues worse. Both when he is there and when they finally dump him back out to the canals, where he'll feel worse than before and not be as strong. And the doubt—" She blinked.

"Is there any way you can, you know, petition his release to the Seats?" Dime had no idea if there was such a process. Even for hemsa, the Circles offered an appeal process, though it was unevenly applied and often too slow.

"No." Volana turned her head to one side and then back. "I've tried before. Our regional clerk only explains to me how dangerous tzetz is." She held up a hand. "Before we discuss Uchitar, I need you to know there is more." She paused, as if watching to ensure everyone had dropped that chain of thought. "The other news, I learned before I left the previous place. It is about our friend, Rock."

Dime tensed. *Rock?* What could Rock have done that would have reached as far as the Underground? Maybe they didn't keep quite as isolated as they claimed. Either way, it was serious enough for Volana to risk flying through the heart of Lodon. Dime encouraged her on, pushing away her own new flutters.

"Or at least I think it is. There is a rumor that a Circles pyr, they called her an 'agent named Rock,' was caught inside the Sol's Pillars, pretending to join them for information. I don't know how they decided who she was; the solies were uncomfortable discussing it with me. But the Sol's Pillars are keeping her with them."

"Keeping her?" Dime said it aloud. "What do you mean, *keeping her?*"

After her initial shock, Dime did recall that the last time Rock had been "arrested" it had been her own ploy to gather information. Yet, still. Rock had pissed Jaza off something fierce, and who knew what either of the fe'pyrsi would do given the opportunity.

As for this idea of Rock being kept somewhere—sure, Ja-lal would drive unwanted pyrsi away, but holding them in a place—if Rock were truly being held somewhere, that *would* cause rumors to fly. Of course solies would be uncomfortable discussing it.

If Jaza had Rock somewhere against her will, Dime wasn't going to let that stand. As frustrated as she felt with Rock, well—

She had a vague sense the others had restarted the discussion around her, but Dime continued to parse through Rock's options. Rock now knew she could use soly valence, and having used it in a place as amplifying as the diamond caves—maybe that would give her a boost in its understanding.

Couldn't Rock use her valence to get out? To create a gap through enclosures, or use enhanced hearing to develop a plan? Maybe Rock wasn't scared enough to push it out of her the way she had when her life had been at risk. The way Dime had outside of the gates, or even during the initial escape. And Rock didn't have a diamond to assist her. Dime had at least seen how fairy valence worked; Rock would be guessing. Going against a lifetime of assumptions.

Dime couldn't assume anything either. Even if Rock could escape with her valence, she was smart enough to know what the consequences could be. Breaking through their doors, if they had secured them, would be the Violence and could set their flame alight with a whole new string of propaganda. She could frighten the Sol's Pillars further, inciting them to more drastic means. Or—revealing Ja-lal valence might be an asset Rock wasn't ready to provide them.

Yet, Volana hadn't come here upon learning of rumors of Rock. She'd come here after hearing about Uchitar. Arrest was a standard practice in her culture, one having nothing to do with Volana and Dime's aims of building support for reconnecting the two societies. Uchitar was in prison per their established laws. Volana didn't care. She wanted to help her friend. Because she loved him.

If that was a mistake, then Dime might make the same mistake with Rock.

But. All she'd had these past cycles to keep her going had been the love and support of her friends. What would she have without them? She hadn't told anyone here that she and Rock had argued; Volana probably assumed Rock had left with other business. She didn't even know if her friend, a remarkably skilled agent, was in trouble, but could she take that risk?

And what if she did? Finally, after all the running and hiding and back and forth and after working through her fears and hang-ups, Dime and her friends had a plan. They were ready to move out. They couldn't just abandon that now, for friends who may even be safe. Except, she didn't think they were safe. An image of Rock crossed her mind: the fear Rock had shown when she almost died there, in the caves. When Dime had hurt her.

She saw Volana's eyes and the worry in them. She remembered

the owl, sitting silently in her borrowed room. In her own pocket, the small wooden charm that she'd shown to no one else.

Then she remembered what Ella had said. What Ador had said. What Batu had been trying to tell her, here. All since the beginning— this didn't have to be about her. Batu had said it, hadn't she? We all help in our own ways?

They were all staring at her. "You're . . . alright?" Ador fidgeted.

Dime understood. She supposed after her last bouts with valence they didn't want her cracking the tower floor or something. She tried to don a settling smile, but she was pretty sure it just came off strange. She dropped the smile.

"I'm sorry, I've been thinking."

"We could see that," Batu said.

"Yes. Well. I think we proceed as planned. Except . . ." The fact was, they'd already delayed too long and it was unclear when a turning point would be reached when the Violence would return and not abate. Dime's blood chilled at the thought.

"I think that you should continue with the plan, at least for now. Ador, you work with the Free Winds and tell them what you've seen and what else has happened. You'd be better at it than me, anyway. And Volana, you work with the Foundry. Spread the message. The two of you can stay here a few bells first, if you want. Strategize and ensure the message is being communicated consistently across both lands."

Knowing she had excluded herself, they all waited. Dime took a breath. "I'll go get the others. And I'll be back soon."

"No," Ador protested. "We'll all go together."

Volana threw a hand into the air. "I am going to help Uchitar; I just needed you to know before I did. If anything happened to me, you'd need a new partner in the Heartland. And here, I could tell you about Rock as well. And help find her, later, if I could."

Dime waved both of her hands. "Please, listen. Ador, you'll be moving on the ground, as we do here. I mean, you know, walking and toothcars, sorry, I made it sound weird. My point is, Volana will be flying in the forest. The familiar sight of each of you will ease pyrsi in, for these first discussions. I'll be there later. Please."

"Dime," Batu offered in a coaxing tone. "Have you considered that in either case, they might be hoping you'll go there yourself, so they can . . . take you also?"

She froze, considering whether that could be true. In Jaza's case, certainly. Would Neimano know about Uchitar? They'd been seen together at the gathering. Her eyes met Batu's. "They might be."

"Diamond." She turned to see Volana, her eyes glowing almost like the fairy stones themselves. "You are not in charge of me."

Embarrassed, Dime hastened to agree. "Of course not, Volana. I didn't mean to suggest that. I just know how good you are at talking to pyrsi, and you fit in there, and—"

Volana raised a finger. "Where were you going to go first?"

"To Uchitar," Dime said without hesitation. "Rock is one of the most capable pyrsi I've ever met, and I'm not even certain how much danger she's in; Uchitar, we know is suffering."

Volana's expression softened and she lowered her hand. "I agree. I don't know if Rock is safe either, but I do know Uchitar will suffer. Again. And . . . alone. I am going to him soon, regardless. If you insist on going, I would be grateful for that help. If things go well, I can be right back to work and you can go to find Rock." She paused. "If they don't, we'll all be arrested, perhaps for a very long time. You need to know that."

"I do." Dime sighed. She had no intent of being arrested, but she wasn't sure she wanted to say it. Volana was right about the risk and that was the point. "I want to go find him and get him out. If the Seats don't like it, it will be the least of their concerns. Ador, did I boss you around too?"

"You tried." Ador grinned. "Circles culture," he said to Volana. "It gets in your mind."

Dime bristled, but Ador had switched tone.

"I was actually planning on visiting your friend Ella once I got back," he said, "after all, it seems she's been involving herself. But

I can try to find your friend first, or at least I can use our network to—"

"No." Dime caught herself. "What I'm saying is I think I should find Rock. I understand her. And she'd hate to have the whole Free Winds out looking for her, for a whole lot of reasons. If it's ok, I'll go after Rock. As soon as Uchitar is out." She thought a moment. "Talking to Ella does seem like a good idea. There's no reason you still shouldn't go. While Volana and I go to Pito." Ador would slow them down in the Heartland, and he knew that.

Ador nodded. "I should be able to find her tower. I've met Ella before, in the city, though no one has seen her for a while. She has the best sources in all of Sol's Reach, when she wants to. She's a legend, among the pyrsi who care to know her."

Volana was tapping one index finger slowly atop the other. She looked up, her eyes wistful. "Is Ella far away?"

"No," Dime answered. "A couple bells—your spans—by foot. Much quicker by flight."

Volana grimaced as if weighing options. "If it's alright with both of you, I would like to go there first. We need to get to Uchitar before his next phase, but a brief delay won't matter. I had a nice conversation with Ella after the gathering at the commons, and I was concerned for her after what happened there. I felt she had difficulty."

Dime had worried about Ella also, but now that everyone seemed to know where Dime was, she'd not wanted to draw the Circles or Sol's Pillars attention to her friend. Yet if Volana was planning on going anyway—

"I'll drive," Ador said.

Dime thought for a moment. "Volana and I will go separately, and I'll take my chair. We'll arrive first, and then, if we need to, we can leave. Hopefully we'll still be there when you arrive." She walked over to where Ador had set the map and brought it back to the low table between the couches, opening just the section wes of the city. "It's right about here. A four-story mini-tower. You don't see it until you're basically there, but if you miss it, you can stay along the first ridge and you'll see it." A memory tickled at her.

"Oh." Dime got up and went back into the guest room, bringing out one of Ella's flares. "If you can't find her, you can use this. We'll come out and find you."

"I shouldn't need it, but thanks."

"And you'll be fine, driving by yourself?" Dime didn't want to get into what had happened at Hin's home downstairs, but she knew he'd been relying on Hin to help him drive. Pedaling alone taxed Ador's aging legs.

"I'll be fine," Ador replied. Then, more pointedly, "I'll be back to settle things with him soon." By his grimace, he wanted no more of that conversation. She could see how upset Ador was, and understood, with the amount of care he'd extended toward the younger pyr. Batu had told her more about Hin's background, and the difficulty he'd had before leaving his village. Pyrsi were rarely just one dimension. There was always a story. Still, he'd have to decide.

Batu adjusted her seat. "Volana, if you ever need anything in Lodon, fly right here. I'm often here, even when Ador is out, and if I'm at classes, please let yourself in. Now that you've seen which deck is ours, land right there and make yourself at home."

Ador drummed his fingers over the map, turning to Volana. "We've kept Batu's role more . . . quiet on purpose. But if anyone doubts her contributions, their misunderstandings would be grave."

"It takes everyone, in a coalition," Volana said.

Dime loved to listen to the fairy speak, which is one of the reasons she wanted her in front of the movement in the Heartland. For a pyr who was always reminded of her supposedly low-class role in fairy society, her every word rang in Dime's mind as part of a grander vision. Here, Dime was just some escaped agent, stumbling to make any difference, and falling over herself at a few harsh words. Volana was a *light*. Pyrsi would listen to her; Dime felt sure of it. She'd known it from the moment she'd met her.

Volana sat straighter. "A coalition is like any effective team. It takes all the voices, direct, coaxing, and even whispering, to spread a message. All are valuable; none should be discounted. Each of us, we have a contribution to make. We are here. We are ready. And so will be our friends, when we find them and offer them our hands."

The group stood, as if they were all ready to bolt through the staircase together. Batu, who had remained seated, leaned forward. "When is the last time you have rested?"

Dime had rested a good deal during her time back; Batu knew that. Glancing at her friends, she saw what Batu meant. Volana and Ador had just made the long journey from the Underground. Ador by toothcar—and even with Hin's help driving, Ador was not growing younger. And Volana, carrying the weight of her pregnancy, and having to ascend the space between the tall upcity towers, trying to find the right one, along with the fear of being seen. Volana's eyes bore dark circles and Ador's shoulders drooped, despite their padding.

"I suggest you allow yourself to sleep," Batu said. "I know that's difficult, knowing friends are at risk. But you'll do them no good without your own strength restored. At least a bit. Dime, you would allow Volana to use the second bed?"

"Of course." Dime glanced nervously at Volana, not knowing if she could sleep knowing her friend was being held. But Volana had offered to go to Ella's first. Dime would trust her sense of the situation.

Volana did not argue, and soon Dime had nestled back into her bed, with Volana on the other side of the room. It was only a moment before a light snoring filled the space, the fairy's wings fluttering with each breath. The rhythm was calming, and soon Dime drifted off.

Interlude

Ji'Hark was going to die. Ve didn't want to die, in the grand scheme of life, but now that ve believed it would be soon, ve'd embraced the idea.

For turns now, ve'd met with family members: vis children, their children, with *their* children in tow. Ve'd offered them each a special gift—something ve thought they'd like, or a choice of items if ve wasn't entirely sure. One of Hark's children had received vis stained-glass necklace. Another had received the family portrait they'd had painted, so many cycles ago. And vis youngest just wanted Hark's storybook, with hand-lettered tales, penned down over the course of a lifetime.

A lifetime that was about to end. It had been at least ten turns now since Hark had left vis home and started the long climb into the mountains. Ve couldn't say exactly why ve'd done it, and most of vis family didn't understand either. But ve didn't want the others to see vis decline. And still having some semblance of strength in vis limbs, ve felt ve was given a gift. And ve was going to take it.

The hike here had been cleansing. Ve'd almost turned back on the long paths through Nor Lodon, but as ve moved away from the outlying homes, ve felt a new connection to the solitude. There were creatures here, of course, but the creatures did not bother ver; they went on their own ways just as Hark went on vis. And, eventually, Hark had immersed verself in the peace of this rocky, harsh land. The colors. The sounds. The howling of the wind, like a final dirge.

The last turn had been the most difficult. The pain in vis throat had grown to a new severity, like the medic had told ver it would. Ve could hardly eat the food ve'd brought, and a knot of deep hunger was growing now too. The medic had given ver strong herbs to deal with it, on a promise ve wouldn't leave them where anyone else could get to them. Finally, ve'd pulled them out and chewed them, one by one.

As she'd told ver, the herbs, once taken, had a strong effect. Ve felt more disconnected now, even the pain felt like something outside of ver. Something to look at but not to experience. Vis limbs were no longer stable, though. They shook and wobbled, and ve couldn't find the right placement on the steep, rocky ground.

So, ve knew, it was time to find the right spot. Or, maybe, like vis life, there never was a right spot, but just a good spot. Good enough.

Vis mind was clouding now. Ve shuffled up a rocky patch, trying not to slip, and glad for the thick canvas gloves. For bells, ve'd been enjoying the peace of the skystones and the long, peaceful night, but ve was not upset now that it was daylight again. Sol's light streamed down, warming vis skin, even brighter than in vis home.

Ve took one long, last look. The place ve'd chosen looked out on a valley. There was a gathering of scruffy trees, and a huge furry barip, who rose on hind legs to see what Hark was doing. Birds soared by. Just then, Hark saw a gathering of prickly orange flowers. Staring at them, slowly vis eyes drifted shut, yet the flowers remained. And Sol's light.

And most of all, the pyrsi who had loved ver.

Act 2

Choices

Volana flew gracefully with broad strokes of her shimmering wings as Dime propelled herself forward in her patched-together wooden chair. Dime's backpack was again closed into the storage space behind her, though she'd left many of her bulkier items, including the owl, back in Batu's guest suite.

"This way," Dime called. She'd taken a high and winding path at first, one that avoided the outgate villages, but here as they approached the old woods, they lowered and descended in a more direct route. Dime continued to glance at Volana with concern. In the forest, fairies flew in low, short bursts. Flying so high over the hills, they'd not been able to take many breaks to rest, and she figured Volana must be tired, especially after her long flight from Pito. Yet, not wanting to be seen, Volana had insisted they push.

Together, they lowered amongst the spiky trees, and Ella's tower popped into view. Dime set the chair down just outside the door as Volana landed into a crouch beside her. "Ella," Dime called, not wanting to startle her. Unlike homes in the city, Ella's door didn't have a privacy turner. So Dime was never sure if she was interrupting her sleep.

Volana looked around at the trees, her eyes wide. Streaks of dark shadow crisscrossed her robes and her wings behind her.

"This is called the old woods," Dime said as she stood. "Oh . . . and your dining chair is a short flight that way." She waved toward the hut. "Sorry. It's out of the rain, and I'll make sure you get it back." She'd left it on the side where the roof was still intact, which she'd hoped was safer than continuing to tug it around.

"No worries," Volana answered, now staring up at the tower.

Dime chuckled to herself. With the fairy's perception of Dime, the fact that she'd left her dining chair in a strange soly woods didn't even faze her. "Ella," Dime called again as they walked forward.

Ella opened the door just before they reached it. Her surprise at seeing them was soon overtaken by a warm smile. The ground floor, mostly for storage and with passage to the bath, had a rather pungent odor. She saw Volana's brows rise in her peripheral vision.

"It's pickles." Ella pointed to a wood barrel. "Was just bringing them in." She was wearing a thick apron, which appeared to be freshly stained with juice. Removing it, Ella hung the fabric over a hook, revealing a simple ecru shirt and a pair of baggy pants. Ella's collage of tattooed leaves poked out from the collar and ran over her head and neck.

"Are they ready to eat?" Volana asked. She dipped her nose over the bucket then pulled away, grimacing.

"Yes, would you like one?"

Seeing their tentative nods, Ella retrieved a metal spear and used it to hand a dripping green pickle to each of her guests. "Need to mop anyway."

Despite the pungency of the brine, the pickle itself was mild, yet infused with a deep herbal quality and only a hint of sweetness. With no elegant way to bite the overlarge pickle and keep the brine off of her clothes, Dime angled awkwardly over the tiled floor.

"Another?" Ella had already speared a third pickle, this one orange, perhaps an orangeroot, and handed it to Volana. Dime started to wave to say she'd had enough, but then saw Ella hadn't offered her one.

As they walked up the curved stairs to the living area, Volana praising the beauty and design the whole way, Dime was glad to rinse her fingers off in the raised basin. She relaxed back into Ella's chair, thinking now that she should have campaigned for one of those orange pickles.

"Go ahead and put them on," Ella said. "I still broom by the spans. Habit, I suppose."

Dime was confused until she saw Volana take out her tree shoes. Not quite able to bend forward, Volana shimmied her boots off next to the stairwell, where they landed with an almost polite *thunk*. She slipped on the smaller shoes, with noticeable relief at the familiar practice.

Ella pulled another chair out from next to a cabinet and ran a towel over it, first the wet side and then the dry side. As she offered it to Volana, Dime noticed that the chair had a curved yet almost triangular back, allowing Volana's wings to rest naturally over the wood while still providing her support. They each took a seat, facing each other around the round table.

Normally, at this point, she'd expect Ella would be curious how things had gone on their recent visit to the Underground. But then, Ella had been uncomfortable talking about it, something Dime now understood. She was unsure where they should start.

Volana set her hands together. "We have returned from our destination, and Dime and I have something we've decided to do. But first, I was thinking about you. After our conversation at the commons, I wanted to see whether you were well."

Ella's wrinkles deepened. "It's been difficult for me lately. But I will get by. And your checking on me here ... it already helps. Would you tell me what thing you are going to do?" Ella pointed at Dime. "Her exploits keep me amused."

Dime glared but Ella ignored her.

"My friend, Uchitar, was arrested for using tzetz," Volana said. "He was in a vulnerable place already, and I fear for him there. We are going to retrieve him. He will manage for now, but I want to get to him before his awareness sets in."

Ella straightened. "You are going to break someone from the dead caves?" She inhaled sharply, turning to Dime as if questioning her wisdom. Well, she shouldn't blame her, anyway. Volana had been going to go without her. Dime was just tagging along.

"Hey, I've done it before," Dime offered, trying to back Volana up. "When I went into the diamond caves to learn valence, I got Rock out." They'd discussed the caves at length when she'd visited Ella afterward, but they hadn't talked about the piece with Rock. "And she was in one of the cages. Uchitar's just in the back part. The prison?" She thought that's what they'd called it.

"Rock? The lovely pyr I met at commons? She's a *Ja-lal.*" Ella sounded exasperated. "The Seats were probably glad you removed her." Ella tapped the table. "Even if not, you risked your welcome in a land not your own. For Volana," she waved across at her, "she risks everything she's ever known."

"It is mine to risk," Volana said in a soft voice.

"Well, so it is." Ella sat back. "And then what?"

"Then we are going to do what you did." Volana's chin took a defiant rise. "We are going to be brave and show ourselves in both lands. We will be seen."

"*Mmm.*" Ella didn't seem to be reacting to that the way Volana had hoped. Dime thought she understood.

"I've been struggling with those thoughts, too." Dime didn't want to call Ella out, but she'd also struggled with this odd feeling that living your life and making the choices that you could somehow wasn't enough. "We can't put out our own lamps worrying about what we have and haven't done. It's not that simple."

Volana seemed to take her meaning, and she shifted in her seat, turning back to Ella. "I think what you did was brave. I think you've always been brave."

Ella tossed her hand. "No, no, I didn't take it bad. I agree that events have brought us to a juncture. Maybe one we couldn't leap before, but now an opportunity we're not going to let slip by. I agree. It's why I went." She still wasn't meeting the others' eyes.

It bothered Dime how much the events had worn on all of them. Dime spent half of each bell convincing herself she was worth a chip. Volana, she'd come here for a final tea almost as if she expected to be arrested later. And Ella wouldn't even look them in the face. Yet these were two of the most caring, brilliant pyrsi she'd ever met.

"Can I just say something?" Dime waited, and Ella finally glanced over. "I'm really grateful for both of you. I know this has been a strange set of turns and I don't know where it leads, but I know I wouldn't know how to travel it without you. Without the pyrsi I've met."

"Well." Ella blinked. "If I'm going to send you two out to defy the Seats, can I at least make you something to eat?"

Dime caught Volana's gaze. "Are you worried about the time?"

"I am worried every flap that he is in that place. But he will stay in his haze for now. With a small meal, we can make sure Ador arrives safely before we leave. That would reassure me."

Ella looked surprised.

"Yes, I was actually just going to mention that," Dime hastened to say. "If you don't mind setting an extra place, Ador said you hadn't connected in a while."

"He's coming here?"

"Is that alright?" Dime hoped she hadn't given Ador bad advice.

"Yes, that's fine. It will be nice." She grinned. "You know, as naïve as you were when I first ran into you, it was somehow no shock that you were friends with Ador. Of course you were." She walked over to where Friend draped over a window ledge. "Our world works in the strangest ways." Ella touched her fingers to the side of the plant.

Volana nodded solemnly.

Dime wasn't sure if they'd be comfortable discussing Dayn's continued presence in the Underground or what he was doing there, but she did want to make sure Ella knew the latest on the newts. "Ador did bring me some unexpected news." Ella hadn't turned around, so Dime continued. "Luja and Tum . . . went on their own to the Beds."

Ella turned around.

"I know! I had nothing to do with it. Dayn had some fairies fly them there on a blanket and then he stuck Ador with telling me about it. I mean, Tum loves it there. She talks with the newts as well as you do." Better, really, but there was no point in adding that. And with the use of valence, something Dime didn't have the energy to get into for now.

"Do you . . . do you think it was a good idea? For them to go there? With everything so tense?" Dime trusted Volana, but she'd promised herself to keep the newts' secret as tight as possible for now. She'd already told Batu, mostly because she hadn't wanted to put Ador in a position to keep secrets from his spouse. And so far, no Fo-ror knew.

Not responding at first, Ella wrung her hands. "As I said, the world works in strange ways. Tum's and Luja's instincts are not illuminated by age, nor are they clouded by it. And, really, they're already there?" Ella shrugged. "Trust Dayn."

"That's what Ador said too," Dime mumbled, mostly to herself.

"See, I told you. A wise ma'pyr." With that, Ella hefted a wide-rimmed pot onto the stove.

They had finished eating and were discussing whether they should go search for Ador when they heard the grinding of a toothcar pull up atop the ledge. It was such an unfamiliar sound in the lone tower that everyone fell silent. They turned toward the eas window, where a few trees striped the view of the ledge, bordered with a glimpse of the dark sky beyond.

As Ella went to greet him, Dime almost rose. But, what, did Ella need help answering her own door? She sat back and watched with anticipation as familiar careful steps ascended the winding staircase. Ador entered the living space, Ella close behind.

"I found it," he said, a lilt to his smile.

Ella snorted, walking around to face him. "I appreciate your respect toward my secrets, but you knew where it was the whole time; did you tell them you'd have to search for it? Do these two still think you don't know *everything*?"

"I have no doubt," Volana said before returning to the herbal tea Ella had steeped for her. She hadn't even asked Dime her preference, knowing Dime's intense fondness for Ella's roasted brew, a cup of which rested now between Dime's hands.

Ella offered Ador a seat at the table before ladling him a bowl of the rich, warm stew. A dwindling bowl of whipped boughfruit cream sat on the counter, and Ella brought it over, offering him a dollop with a flick of her hand.

Watching the cream melt down into the stew, Dime almost asked for another serving. Even in her most difficult moods at least the joy of eating was not taken from her.

"Stop staring at my stew. I'm sure you had some."

Ador's grin was entirely innocent and Dime rolled her eyes.

Volana rose from the table. "I have rested, I have been fed, and I have enjoyed the company of my best friends." The gleam held back a tiny bit in her eyes, which Dime suspected was not actually for Uchitar, but for missing the pyr she was dating, Eytanii. "Now I must help wonderful, strong Uchitar remember that he is."

For someone who was always talking herself down for her low Fo-ror class, Dime noted the way Volana confidently declared their mission underway.

"I'll be thinking of you both," Ador said, the intensity of his gaze showing how much he meant it. "And Ella, if it's well with you, I'd like to stay and talk a while."

"It would be my pleasure," she said with a bow. "Not quite as much as my friend Dayn you must understand—I hear you are close—but I will make do."

To Dime's surprise, Ador laughed loudly. "So he's won you over? He's still working on me. One of these turns." With a chuckle,

Ador started to tell a story about Dayn and card night and an incident with a huge cake. It was a good story, though not one Dime would have picked for the seriousness of the moment. Ella didn't seem offended.

"Let's go," Volana whispered, bending down to reach Dime's ear. "He's distracting her."

"Oh. Right." She fanned her fingers at Ella, who called back a quick goodbye as she continued to listen to Ador's story. Volana shuffled back into her boots, collapsing the tree shoes into a pocket.

Just as Dime turned to leave, Ador's eyes caught her. "Be well," he mouthed. Dime slipped into the stairwell. Turning back, she tapped the pocket where her dice rested, and Ador smiled.

She and Volana had worked on the plan over the meal, and so without any additional discussion, Dime strapped into her chair and launched up. Volana crouched down and joined her in the air, flapping past and in the direction of the Heartland.

An odd aspect about the Seats' complex being shrouded in Fo-ror reverence was that, unlike the Circles' complex in norside Lodon, the scruffy brush up and along the Great Cliff was always empty.

Even now in the daylight, Dime wasn't too concerned flying down into a small clearing, where she nestled her chair back into a bush as Volana landed beside her. Staring at her backpack a moment, she decided to leave it, instead taking out the pouch Volana had packed with supplies for Uchitar.

As she and Volana had discussed, pyrsi believed the main entrance to be the only way in and out of the complex. Now that Dime knew of one exit further down the cliff, she suspected there were others. And that was another reason they'd walked the last stretch—the guards here were used to pyrsi landing in the extended clearing leading to the arched walkway. No one walked here through the forest.

They stopped just behind the first line of trees. Volana whistled in surprise behind her. "Does it normally look like this?" she asked. "I've never been here."

"You never flew by, just for curiosity?" Even in Lodon, burgesses would wander past the complex, whispering and pointing. They held the power of the Circles as no lesser, but viewed the whole institution as more absolute rather than sacred.

"No." Volana seemed taken aback by the suggestion. "What reason would I have to draw the Seats' attention?" She paused. "I've known pyrsi assigned to work here. Stories are common. Stories, privately, in our homes."

Dime peered out from behind a wide trunk and was surprised, though perhaps she shouldn't have been, to see at least a dozen guards surrounding the main entrance, including one High Guard, though she didn't recognize xem. Neimano wasn't looking to be surprised by her again, she supposed. Good, she didn't want to see him either.

Carefully, they drew back and Dime circled them around, up over the edge of the hill. "I should warn you. The side door is by the compost. It stinks."

"I have smelled worse than compost," Volana said, as she followed Dime down to the side wall.

Glancing to check that no one was watching, Volana flapped over the hedge. Dime started to squeeze through, then stopped, shaking her head. With a wave, she gently bent the branches to each side and slipped through the jagged opening, the leaves rustling into place as the branches closed behind her.

"Ok, look for an interesting stone."

Volana scrunched her face. "That is not specific."

"It's like, this big, and curled around sort of like a bean, but you can't see the bean because I buried it a little, so it's really more like a knob. But it had some spots."

Volana trudged off, folding her wings tightly behind her as she edged down the narrow space between the long hedge and the roughly-finished wall. The wall, covered in plaster, was not made of the stone cliff but was built from a structure emerging from it. Dime had thought about coming in this way before, when she'd rescued Rock, but she wasn't familiar with valence then so she'd been nervous to risk it. Now she felt no qualms. Sometimes, realizing how quickly her own sentiments had changed, she felt disoriented.

Speaking of which, she stopped, concerned she'd gone too far along the wall. She turned back to see Volana had folded her arms.

"You are good at valence."

"Thanks?" Dime had no idea if she was good, though she did have some oomph to it. And here, she could sense the diamond caves, as if they noticed her, remembered her. She felt powerful—and tried to subdue that feeling as best she could. She wanted to open the door but didn't want to light a virtual flare that she was here.

"If you've connected with an object you may be able to call it," Volana continued. "Can you try imagining the stone in your mind?" She smiled politely. "Also, please hurry. You were right—this smell is rancid like my mother's bog boots. Ma-mi, not Ma-ma," she clarified, clearly not wanting to disparage her mother whose boots did not smell.

Dime pulled her shoulders back, suddenly aware of the static layer of anxiety that she carried. Anxiety clouded her valence; it clouded her. She tried to shake the tightness away, mentally as well as physically, but it did not leave. Frustrated, she searched for a calmer place, like an open tower garden at the end of a sky alley. She continued to walk, figuratively, until she was alone in a clearing. Here, she could reach out, along the wall, along the soil, and ask the stone where it was. The anxiety had not left her, but she had left it—in the figurative room behind.

The stone wasn't far. She lifted it, and it hovered in the air, where she could see it spinning slowly as she opened her eyes. "There," she said, pointing. Knowing she'd need valence to open the door and not knowing what they'd find inside, she tried not to look at Volana or otherwise let the outside world back in. Not quite yet.

She walked to the door, completely imperceptible against the textured wall. But she knew it was there and she drew her hand over, letting the hinges swing open. With relief, she sensed nothing unusual inside, and stepped through. Once into the passageway, she lit the glowstones, waiting until Volana had entered to shut the door behind them. She allowed a long, deep breath, and then exhaled.

Volana's brows were raised. "You are as skilled as any trained caster. You really only started recently?"

"I started a long time ago, I think. I just started *this* now."

"So we are in the complex?" Volana's wings were pulled back tightly against each other, a posture Dime had learned indicated nervousness.

"Yes. If you want, I'll get him. I'm already under arrest; it's less risk to me." She kept her voice calm, trying to reassure Volana she really could wait here, or return outside.

"I'm going with you." Volana stepped ahead, moving a hand over her midsection.

Dime followed, whispering behind her. "So we'll try to stay away from view. I'd rather avoid a confrontation if possible. But, you know, it's not likely."

"We'll do what we must. If I'm imprisoned, at least I can care for him."

Yes, she'd worried that Volana had figured she'd be caught and arrested. Dime had no intention to be. Either way, she trusted Volana would give her best effort. The part that concerned her was knowing how strictly the Fo-ror followed their Seats. But Volana was in the Foundry. And she was here. Whether she'd openly defy an order from a guard was a different question.

They reached the end of the passage, and Dime lifted up a hand. "This is it. Once through here, they'll be able to see us. If one of us can get out, then we do it. Agreed?"

"Agreed," Volana said.

With a wave, the lights turned off. And Dime opened the door, out into the loud hallway near the kitchen area. A huge kitchen, rooms and rooms, as it sounded like from all the bustle.

"You go along the wall," Volana said. Raising her wings behind her and rising naturally taller than Dime, Volana marched along, as if she walked this way every shift, and mostly blocking Dime from view as they passed pyrsi on their way through the corridors.

Remembering how she'd found the stone, Dime tried to calm herself, focusing her valence on the complex itself. Reconnecting with the caves and the stone that surrounded them. And soon she could sense the layout, feel which way to go.

She began to whisper each turn to Volana as they wound through. Without warning, Volana swung around, chattering what sounded to Dime like nonsense as her wings spread wide.

"Hey, watch where you're going," a pyr muttered.

"Sorry," Volana called after xem.

She shrugged. "Xe passed too close. I wanted no chance."

It was funny that, at least for now before she started speaking publicly, Volana was nothing of note here. Though she had a reputation out in the canals and among those who looked down on them, here she was simply common, with her lanky gait and pieced-together robes. Just a pyr wandering the halls, probably on her way to shift.

Hiding a soly behind her wings.

"The dead caves are this way." Dime motioned, and together they stepped into what Dime thought of as the office area, seeing rows of pyrsi sitting at desks, writing on paper or huddled together, designing plans. Reviewing deliveries, maybe. Dime knew the Seats decided who got what food and supplies, and supposed someone had to work it out.

They walked past what was clearly a commode, as a pyr stepped out rubbing xyr hands on xyr robes. Volana cringed.

"Yeah, this is sort of the backstage tour," Dime noted. "The Seats' main areas are really fancy. I'll show them to you sometime if I can. But, you know."

Dime had gone this way for a few reasons. Mostly, she thought these offices, with their bustle and busy pyrsi, would be easier to walk through unnoticed. Second, and less comfortable to consider, she didn't want to see those cages again. She simply didn't. And she knew this entrance, which she didn't think was even marked as an entrance, bypassed the diamond-laced cages where she and Rock had been detained.

"It's here," Dime whispered as they approached a dark section of corridor. Not seeing anyone behind them, Dime waved her hand and, as before, the wall itself swung open. With a hop, they were back in the dreary gray tunnels, stained with darker marks, like char.

"This is the dead caves?"

"Yes, part of it." Dime glanced around. "Sort of the outer part." She hesitated. "Closer to the diamond caves."

"Why isn't it guarded? I can understand why pyrsi wouldn't try to leave, but I'd think they'd want to make sure no one wandered back here who wasn't allowed. Especially, well, you."

Volana had a point. But, she figured, the front entrance had been heavily guarded and perhaps Neimano had figured even Dime couldn't get past that gaggle unnoticed. Or they were here, waiting for her.

"Maybe they don't think you'll keep coming back," Volana offered.

Yes, or maybe that. Dime did have to wonder. Still, knowing no one wandered the dead caves unless they had to and they shouldn't be in the path of the guards, she felt they could stop and relax a stride. "The cages I told you about are that way." She pointed. "I don't want to see them, if you don't mind. That way," she moved her arm, "is the passage to the diamond caves. And right in front are the majority of the dead caves, which sound like they've been cleared out of all the diamonds. I've never actually been back that way, into the standard prison area. Only into the diamond caves."

Volana's gaze toward the diamond caves was wistful. "They must be guarded."

"They are, probably more now." Dime squinted. Something felt different, and she wasn't sure what it was.

"What do you feel?"

"It's . . . well, I don't know. Something that way feels off. Anyway, we should stay away."

"True." She hesitated. "I'm sorry; I just want to see if I'm right. Please, stay here." Not really asking, Volana walked off toward the large door that separated the diamond caves from the rest of the complex. With a start, Dime remembered there'd been a High Guard there. If Volana wasn't back very soon, she'd go and find her.

A few strides later, Volana returned. "It's what I thought. There is a new door close to here, before any physical door, made entirely of valence. You can't see it, but luckily I'm used to walking like this." Volana often held her hands protectively over where her child continued to grow, to prevent inadvertent bumps. "No, don't worry, I could sense it too. You're right; the feeling is so strong." She paused. "I wonder how it's generated."

Dime could start to imagine ways a boundary could be created, similar to what she'd made outside the den. She had no idea how to do that again; her best work always seemed to be when she didn't know what she was doing.

Without anyone holding the barrier, they'd have to charge the stones, she supposed. Good thing they weren't going that way. "So Neimano locked the diamond caves. Must be why he isn't guarding the other doors. Probably figures that's the only place I'd go. *Hmm. I wonder if Ferala knows.*"

Volana winced.

"Sorry," Dime apologized, knowing fairies were simply not used to hearing their leaders discussed by name or in familiar ways. She'd had the same issue back home, casually discussing Sala and the Light's Circle with Ador, but then having other pyrsi be shocked to hear it. Though, he'd never mentioned they'd *dated.* Sol. Now that was familiar.

"Well, let's hope there's no barrier this way." Dime knew what

Volana was thinking, as her friend stepped forward. They both knew there wasn't one. They felt nothing ahead of them.

"So I have no idea how this works." Dime glanced around. "I guess the pyrsi will be back in rooms this way."

"It's disgusting." Volana looked like she was going to be ill. Dime understood; she'd felt the same when she'd first learned about arrest. "It's not just that pyrsi are held here, not being aided but just set aside, but then they make it ugly too."

Dime raised her brows.

"Back there, wood paneling, colorful glass, knobs of pink stone. Here, gray and char. So, what, you want them to follow your rules and so you make them as unhappy as possible? What pyr designed this?"

Dime snorted, though she didn't mean it to be funny. "That wasn't even the fancy part. That was like, the kitchen and the offices." She couldn't imagine Volana seeing the lounge. And Dime herself had only had a peek inside.

They walked forward, peering around for guards, as voices came into hearing ahead. The narrow passage opened into a large, undecorated room with the same natural, drab walls, some sections solid and others crushed stone. It was well-lit with glowstones and there were shelves and cabinets with what looked to be books and games. Pyrsi milled about, seated at tables or leaned against a wall. They quieted as the two fe'pyrsi entered.

"We aren't with the guards," Dime said in a low voice. "We won't tell anyone that you saw us and we hope to leave soon. Is someone named Uchitar here?"

As unusual as Dime must have appeared with soly clothing, short hair, and no wings, they couldn't have been the first visitors, as the groups of pyrsi ignored her question and went back to their activities. She and Volana each scanned the space. No one resembled Uchitar, and no one approached them. Several passages opened from the back, and choosing one, they walked through.

Open areas sprung to each side and up and down a web of

passages. Without curtains, the rooms were open to the walkways, and the only doors were marked with the circle she'd learned marked a washroom here, the way a waterdrop was used in Sol's Reach. The passages were dotted with tray-tables, holding small comforts such as books, notepads, tissues, scents, and lotions. As they walked, Volana softly called Uchitar's name. Finally she stopped. "He's over here."

In a room by himself, Uchitar was curled into a corner atop a mess of blankets, against, but not in, a modest bed. Three other beds rested empty nearby. The room smelled of a strong cleaning solution, and a tray of food sat untouched to one side. Uchitar smelled slightly of vomit, and he was unmoving. Gently, Volana reached down and rolled him over. "We are almost too early," she whispered. "But it is close, and I did not want to be too late. Hopefully he can walk.

"Hey, friend," she said, reaching for the bag Dime still carried. Taking out a flask and a cloth, she dampened the cloth and ran it over Uchitar's face and mouth.

His eyes flew open and he sat up, his eyes alarmingly red.

"Yeah, it's me," Dime said. "And Volana. Still not a dream."

"But I was arrested." His eyes didn't focus on them, as if he weren't fully aware.

"You still are," Volana said. "But we're leaving anyway. We have to save the Heartland, remember? Prevent the Great War?" As before, when they'd first met, Volana motioned to Dime and they leaned him back, coaxing him to sip water from Volana's flask.

"They told me to leave," he said. His eyes rolled back, then adjusted.

"I know. I know." She ran a hand against the side of his cheek. "If you want to get out of here, you'll need to stand. If Dime lifts you by your pants, it will not be so comfortable."

To her surprise, Uchitar chuckled. He reached out a hand, and Volana took it. "Give Dime the other," she said. "My balance is not at its best."

Together, she and Volana hoisted the tall fairy to a wavering stand.

Uchitar staggered between them, his steps labored. Pyrsi in each room ignored the group as they passed, probably wanting to avoid any notice themselves. Perhaps if they assisted, their time here would increase. With that sensitivity, Dime did not look their way.

Finally, they made it back to the door leading to the office area, and Dime swung it open as they guided Uchitar through and around the first few turns. At first, she was relieved to see the way clear. No one waiting for them. Then, stopping together, Dime realized the entire area was empty. No voices came from the row of rooms, no shuffling of papers.

"This isn't good," she said.

"Let's keep going," Volana muttered, fatigue in her tone.

Dime sensed him before she saw him. His presence felt disturbed, like sand against a window, but she was sure it was him. "Neimano is here," she whispered. "I'll deal with him. If you can get out, you get out. That was our deal. I'm going to keep him talking. Here, go." She eased her hand away from Uchitar, cringing as his weight flopped over against Volana's side. "Are you ok?" Volana nodded. Dime raised her voice. "Neimano!" She called out down the hall, then realized Volana had not left. Though, Uchitar would be hard to move on her own. She turned back, but Volana waved her forward.

Neimano appeared around the corner, his black robes twirling around him. His face looked thin and loathing filled his eyes, but he must have recovered from Stern Eyes' valence, at least enough to have returned to the complex. Only one guard flanked him, and it was not Ulkanet. Oddly, Neimano jolted at the sight of Dime, reaching out to grasp the wall's wooden trim. The guard stared at Dime with terror, and Dime realized, xe thought Dime had attacked Neimano in the forest. Did Neimano think so also, or did he blame the newts? Perhaps he felt safe here, in his complex, where any bursts of valence would be immediately investigated.

Though Uchitar had fallen into a daze, with a quick glance to Volana she saw that the fe'pyr was afraid. "He's just a pyr," Dime whispered. "Just like you." She stopped. "No, sorry, you're better." She looked at the powerful pyr, remembering how he'd held her children breathless, how his guard had waved diamond ropes in their faces, and she understood how Stern Eyes had reacted the way she had.

Dime filled with disgust, then determination, then almost reckless anger. A ma'pyr that would harm ch'pyrsi. She would give him no satisfaction.

"You think you can just walk in here?" Neimano's voice was calm but it carried a low growl.

"Is that rhetorical?"

"What?" Neimano sputtered.

"Well, clearly, I think that, Third Seat. Honestly, this is my fourth time literally just walking in here. See. You should give yourself more credit. You know, maybe you picked a good ba'pyr after all." She waved her fingers, in the gesture of the Fo-ror.

Neimano let a breathy hiss. "How did you get in?"

Dime considered implying she'd strolled in the front way, but she didn't want to get any of the guards in trouble. And no way was she putting Ferala's secret passage at risk.

"There are a multitude of ways in and out of the caves, once you understand them."

Neimano paused. Flicking his gaze to his guard, he closed his mouth.

Dime realized she was on to something. He didn't want his guard to know one could leave through the caves. She'd have to remember that. And why was he holding the wall? That was odd. Either way, they couldn't outrun him or the guard, not with Uchitar. Maybe if she could keep him talking she could figure something out.

"So, what's your game, Neimano? I'm not interested in a contest. Really not. You leave us alone, and I'm going to bring the pyrsi back together. All the pyrsi." She was now dedicated to helping the newts as well, but she wasn't going to tip Neimano off to that. "Or are you still set on returning the Violence, have that be your name? You can be remembered for generations just for that. 'Neimano killed.'"

The guard twitched behind him.

"You." Neimano curled his lips. He started to breathe heavily, and Dime wondered if he was recovered after all. "You think I care anything about myself? I care about Sha's pyrsi. I care about the Fo-ror. And I have something you need to—"

He stopped, pivoting unsteadily as another pyr approached. No, two pyrsi, the second calling to the first, behind him. *Three!* Dime knew to stay silent as the three pyrsi with luxurious robes and elegantly styled hair filed in. They strode past Neimano and lined themselves along the hallway, as Neimano released the wall and stood straight.

Ferala stared ahead, as if he'd entered the offices on a whim and hadn't yet noticed anything was happening. Layanie, who had been glaring at Ferala, stopped, vis jaw askew as ve scanned the others. Vis gaze rested on Dime. Dime nodded back, trying to appear respectful. And Tikinal, he stared at his shoes, but she saw his lips tighten.

She understood. It was all too bizarre. But Volana was teetering with Uchitar's weight against her. They had better things to do. All of them did. "With your leave, esteemed Seats, I'm only here to assist my friend. I ask that you forgive my intrusion; it was not done for disrespect. We'll be on our way."

"She broke into the complex," Neimano said, wheezing now. "That is a violation of all of Sha's tradition. She must be arrested and put under restricted security. She defiles Sha; see for yourself."

Seat Layanie, in flowing robes that highlighted vis delicately painted face and tall, sleek figure, turned to Dime. "Why are you here and what is your intent?"

"Honorous Seat Layanie." She waved her fingers, hoping she did it properly enough for a Seat. "I am specifically here on a pyrsonal matter. I know this is not the correct way to enter or petition, but certainly you can see that I would not have been allowed in, and so I did what I felt I needed to do, hoping not to take your valuable time in the process. I mean you no disrespect and I apologize for any disruption.

"My friend, Uchitar, is using tzetz. He does not push; it is his own struggle. He has friends who will care for him in Pito, where he will no longer burden your staff. That is the sole reason I am here, and I respectfully request your permission to leave without incident. But—" Dime, caught by having repeated her respect multiple times, realized what a rare chance it was to have the ear of the two highest Seats. She was not going to let it pass. Dime glanced back at Volana, holding Uchitar like a statue but with hints of strain in her face. *Quickly,* she reminded herself.

"Once we get out, our goal is to establish new avenues between Ja-lal and Fo-ror. To open a dialogue that has long been closed. Despite my feelings that we should do this, I also believe we must. Fo-ror were seen in the city of Lodon. It caused a stir and continues to do so. Then my friend, Ella, showed herself at your gathering, as you are aware.

"Pyrsi on both sides of the cliff continue to talk. I have seen it; they are meeting in larger and larger groups. We must prevent the Violence from returning. We must assure pyrsi that we are of equal value, and to place the opportunity to learn over the instinct to dismiss. We are not so different. Diverse, yes. Flawed—all of us. Some more than others." She tilted her head over at Neimano. "But we're all just living beings trying to be happy and help each other be too."

Layanie seemed to be grasping for a response. Ferala still stared ahead.

Neimano jerked slightly, wavering in place. He braced an unsteady arm against the wall. "She attacked me," Neimano spat, his eyes wide. "Ask her."

Dime froze. He was definitely not well. But he'd asked her directly, in front of Ferala and Layanie, and she feared the implications of a wrong answer—especially with Volana here, struggling to hold Uchitar up. She would not lie and say the attack was hers, nor would she implicate the newts. Yet, relief passed through her. He seemed sincere, though lacking control. He thought she did it. Not the newts. Not Stern Eyes. With this relief, the rest became clear.

"There was a terrible incident, Seat Layanie. Seat Neimano pursued me in the woods, after your speech—why, he must have been in the crowd. And he took my breath with valence, as well as that of my Aoch children. One only a ch'pyr." Volana gasped beside her as Layanie's eyes narrowed. Ferala remained still, though his fists had clenched.

Neimano started to rasp something out, but Layanie silenced him.

"Seat Neimano wishes me to tell the truth," she continued. "I can describe, if you wish, the way my lungs felt, having the air removed from them. Filled with terror for whether my children felt the same. My children—Ji'Luja and Fe'Tum. Those are their names. Ji'Luja studies to be a medic. I am so proud of ver. I wish for them to grow up in a different world, Second Seat. A world where they do not fear the shadow of the Violence or the scream of the Great War. A world where they can sit with fairies like my friend here, and share pots." She almost said *a biscuit*, but then remembered the Fo-ror called meals of sharing *pots*.

"I know that I've disrupted your complex. I also know there is more to this story." She paused. "High Seat Ferala will vouch for that claim."

Ferala moved, only slightly. To his side, Neimano's arm trembled harder against the wall.

"And Seat Neimano, I am worried he is not yet well."

"Enough of this!" Neimano interrupted, his voice shaking. "Some brute bursts into our complex, removes lawfully arrested pyrsi, and you will listen to her like a petitioner! Let me deal with her. I was dealing with her. You have enough to do. *Don't you, Ferala?*"

No. The one thing Dime understood about Ferala was he was a thinker. A maker of slow decisions. She wasn't going to let him be bullied here, where he may weaken her position. Or his own.

"Seat Neimano?" Dime asked, with the tone of a student approaching a busy teacher. As intended, this threw him off.

He turned toward her, still leaning on the wall. "Yes?"

Even in the inherent darkness of the situation, Dime almost laughed. She fixed her gaze on Neimano and spoke clearly. "The mistake I made earlier was thinking you had any power over me. I can't be controlled by you, even by the actions of your own hand, remember? The only way you can do anything to me is if you convince other pyrsi to go along with it." She stepped forward. "And there are more pyrsi who care than pyrsi who do not. You will never win this. So, stop. Just stop."

"Dime!" Ferala interjected. Layanie snapped over to look at him.

"High Seat Ferala," Dime continued, before anyone else could get a word in, "I believe you to be a pyr of good heart. But this has gone on long enough. You know that it has. It is too much of a risk. It is that risk that holds you back; I understand that. But you have vast power, backed by pyrsi who revere you, and you've chosen not to use it to help. I've told you my plan. With all due respect, High Seat, now is the time to hop on board."

Volana was tapping Dime's arm. Whether it was to request she stop provoking the High Seat or a reminder of Uchitar's continued weight, Dime took the cue.

"All I want now is to retrieve this one friend. A single tzetz user can mean nothing to the security of the Heartland. There is no reason to stop me. I mean,"—the absurdity of the whole situation at this point just had her feeling bold—"I'd go in there and march the whole place out, but I can't be sure there isn't someone like Neimano back there and we have enough to deal with for the turn, so I'll stick with this for now. But you should consider it."

"Arrest her," Neimano choked out, now inhaling huge, uncontrolled breaths as one of his legs buckled. His guard shifted, as if unsure whether the command was for xem or an insistence for the higher-ranking Seats.

Dime snorted. "How about don't. I'm no *danger* to your society, only to its stagnation. Besides, even if you arrest me, the message is out there. We've already spread it. It was there before me. Now, because of you, pyrsi are energized to carry it. Pyrsi who will wonder where I've gone. And, besides, I don't intend to let you arrest me. So, what will you do? I ask you again—is your goal to return the Violence?"

She paused, then over the background of Neimano's heavy breathing, she turned to Layanie. "He doesn't answer my question. Now, again, I've taken enough of your time. I promise I am leaving the complex. I just want to take Uchitar and get him to safety. He's important to us." She swept a hand around. "*This* important."

"Who are you?" Layanie had turned away from Dime and was facing Volana. Harm. Dime had been trying to keep her out of this.

"I am Fe'Volana," was all she answered.

"She's brilliant," Dime said, her voice lowering. "Forget her class. You'll be smart to support her. Trust me. Now, please let us leave."

Tikinal looked like he was going to speak. Instead, Layanie stepped forward. "Unless the High Seat objects, I agree that our fragile situation can endure no further disruption. Not here. Not now. I have enough of a mess to clean up." Ve swung over to Dime and Volana. "If I call for you, you will come back. Either of you."

"Yes, your Honorous," Volana answered, adding a slight but sincere-looking bow.

Well, that was done. Dime bowed also.

"You deal with him," Layanie said, swooping off down the hall. Dime didn't look at the remaining Seats, but her eyes strayed quickly to Tikinal. He waved his fingers, and Dime waved back. A warmth settled over her. Then, Tikinal disappeared behind Ferala.

"Dime," Volana was whispering.

Dime reset her grip around Uchitar and hastened to follow after Layanie, Volana at her side and Uchitar bumping between them.

No one spoke as Layanie swung open door after door. Dime

recognized none of these empty halls, one after another. Finally, ve stopped before a flight of stairs.

"If you need entry here again, you will ask. Is that clear?"

"It is clear, Seat Layanie." Adjusting her position against Uchitar, Dime raised a hand to wave her fingers, but instead she paused. "In Sol's Reach, we fan our fingers. Like this." She fanned them. "Like the rays of Sol."

As if twisting vis fingers in a new way, Layanie made the gesture. Yet, vis expression did not soften or change. "Remember what I said. Also, you'll want to be careful at the end of the passage. And I expect you to forget its existence."

Dime did not want to linger, but she wanted this leader to know her intent. "Seat Layanie. I learned a while back not to make promises in generalized absolutes, but I will promise you my only goal is to reduce harm. To all. I will not be perfect; I never have been." She stopped. There wasn't anything more to say.

Volana bowed deeply with whispered words of apology, or perhaps thanks. Soon the Second Seat had disappeared from view.

Dime sighed. "Stairs." She glanced at Uchitar, noting his blank eyes and limp arms. And Volana—Dime regretted how long she'd let her prop Uchitar up. "Sorry about that; I thought you could leave but I didn't think it through."

"This is the least on my mind. You take his feet, I'll take his top." Volana began to heave her arms under Uchitar's. "I'm taller; it makes sense."

Mmm. Keeping her thoughts to herself, Dime hoisted Uchitar's legs as high as she could, and awkwardly, they bumped up the stairs, Uchitar himself taking a few rough swings as they strived to keep him away from Volana's midsection. While Dime worried for Uchitar's health, she wasn't entirely upset that he was unconscious, as this might not be a chapter he'd want to recall. She tried to think how to use valence to carry him, but lifting him without a solid structure might press into him in unintended ways.

And so, together, she and Volana stumbled along, their friend between them. As the path twisted and rose upward, Dime thought only of every step. Every breath. Eventually, she realized that Sol shone upon them again, though she saw no doorway in the ground. Collapsing onto an unforgiving slab of stone, she laid back and groaned.

Pushing herself up one last time, she took what was left in her flask, and coaxed Uchitar to drink it.

"Actually, Uch," she whined, "you probably owe us one."

Dime had tried to talk the fairy out of it, but her logic prevailed, and so, she watched as Volana appeared over the top of the cliff, panting and heaving, guiding Dime's wooden chair in front of her. Dime hadn't seen Volana use valence before, and it seemed to take more effort than Dime herself was used to.

"What do you keep in this thing?" Volana objected as the chair clattered onto the stone. The fairy landed beside it, exhaling.

"Less than I used to," Dime muttered. At least here, in her bag, she had additional food, including some of Batu's herbed crackers. "They should help," she hoped aloud, offering most of the stack to Uchitar, to nibble along with his flask of water.

He'd begun to come to, though not without repeated unpleasant effects. As he did, he mostly cried and moaned. He was rawer than an open wound, and Dime felt uncomfortable, watching such unadulterated pain. Enough that she set aside thinking about whatever she'd done down there. She'd think about it later.

With Volana leaning over him, Uchitar muttered something. Volana looked up, her eyes tired. "He wants me to tell you what happened. He says you deserve to know."

"Oh, no, he—"

"He asked me to tell you." Pulling her knees up, as far as they would go, Volana rocked back against the ground. "He has a spouse, but they do not speak. His children are grown now. He began using in a difficult time. No need for the details. And I cannot fully blame his children, as I was not there with them. I cannot say I've felt what they've felt. Yet, how do I reconcile his pain when he goes back to them, showing that he has changed, or is trying to change, and they force him to leave?"

Dime thought about that. "It must be hard."

"It is always hard. Many things are hard." She turned her head away. That seemed to be the end of the story, for now, and Dime would not press.

They did discuss finding a way to lift Uchitar, but Volana felt sure he'd at least be able to fly again before too long, and distance-wise, they weren't far from Volana's home.

Finally, a groggy Uchitar flapped in brief, wobbly paths, and eventually they helped him through the curtain in Volana's wall. As Dime held him steady, Volana set the cushions back out where he'd been sleeping before. Then, exhausted, they laid him down for rest, while Dime, tired herself but feeling better equipped to wait, sat watch over Uchitar as Volana fell asleep.

Even when Uchitar was awake, he slumped against the wall, his eyes darting at each little sound. Volana steeped a pot of tea. She still hadn't mentioned Dime's speech to the Seats, and Dime was starting to think that she wouldn't.

"The most obvious effects passed while he was in the caves," Volana said. "The shaking and vomiting and severe delusion." She reached into a cabinet, pulling down a tray of cups, and lowered her voice. "That phase is my least concern. He has been through it before, and my presence helps little other than basic care, which they provide him. Yet the effects will run for turns after, making him more and more vulnerable. One moment he'll seem fine, until he feels any sadness or desperation. Then his urge for it will return, like a treefall. Turns and turns of concentration and distraction it takes.

"They say he has no access to it in the dead caves. They don't know that; a little goes far and many have learned to sew doses into their clothing. But even if he didn't, when he doesn't have the substance to turn to, his mind turns into itself. Darkness. Despair. Your own mind, telling you untruths. No one will talk about how a pyr reacts when this happens, but I have seen it. It is this time, after the symptoms have passed to our eyes, that we must most be there to assist him."

She paused, as Uchitar was stirring. He blinked around at the room, as he'd done several times.

"I . . . did you just take me out of there?"

"Umm . . . actually, yeah. We did," Dime said. Next to her, Volana nodded.

The Uchitar Dime knew would have laughed, even if concerned. Instead he rose, wobbling a little. "Need to use the bath." He peered at Volana. "Will be right back. I promise."

If he didn't remember being dragged past the three highest Seats as Dime scolded them, perhaps that was just as well.

A take later, they'd helped him sit up at the counter, and Volana had placed a few pieces of toast in front of him, along with some of the tea.

"I'll be arrested again." He took a bite of the toast.

"No, you won't," Dime said. "We coordinated with the Seats, in a manner of speaking." She and Volana met eyes, and Dime almost caught a grin. "Ferala and Layanie know you left and have accepted it, even if they don't agree with what we did. Neimano has an issue, but it's with me, not you." She gave both of the fairies a look that made it clear she didn't want to talk about Neimano right now. "If he arrests anyone, it would be me. And . . . I don't think that he will." She didn't.

"I have a grandchild," he finally said. "Or, I hoped to."

Volana froze.

He shook his head at her. "I'm fine. Dime deserves to know who she considers part of her movement."

She didn't think of it as her movement, but she wasn't going to correct him like this.

"I've left my children alone. I'm a loser. I've always been a loser. They deserve better than me. Why would I burden them?" He blinked. "Then I heard from someone, at the commons, when we were there. Someone recognized me and asked if I knew about the ba'pyr. Ba'pyr! No, I didn't know. And he's married, too, to . . . a carpenter. Like me.

"I couldn't stop thinking about it. My children deserve better than me, and I knew the ba'pyr should too. But I couldn't stop thinking about the little one. Whether it was fair to xem to not meet a grandparent, when one was right there. I thought, what if the visit is short, and I can just impart the spirit of me? I had done well. I hadn't used in turns. And Dime's movement had me inspired. I felt . . . better than I'd been.

"Volana warned me. She always does. She said she was going somewhere beautiful and new and interesting, and asked me to go with her." Uchitar's jaw set. "What could be more beautiful and new than a tiny ba'pyr! Of your own child? I told her no. Go to your unnamed place yourself and be well. I'll be here when you return."

Sadness grew in Dime's heart, not just for where this was going, but also that Uchitar would have loved the Underground. Yet, here, they weren't allowed to even tell him about it.

"So I went there, to my child's home," he continued. "I didn't surprise him. He didn't deserve that. He knew I would be there, as did his spouse. I rang the chime, and no one answered. Finally his spouse came to the door. Alone. He was polite, but said I was not welcome. He seemed sad." Uchitar started to pick up the tea, but his hand shaking, the cup dropped, shattering as it landed.

Uchitar started to reach for the sharp shards of pottery, but Volana waved an arm and swept them away with valence. Seeing what she'd done, Dime pulled the liquid off the counter, channeling it in a stream down the basin's drain. She gathered the shards into a tight pile, lifting and setting it on a side table until they could bury it outside. Volana rose and began to pour another cup.

"See? She gives me false hope." He clutched his elbows. "She says I can be a normal pyr, but I can't. I couldn't then. I couldn't even see my ba'pyr. So I went to the thicket and—"

Volana turned on her heels. "I have heard enough and so has Dime. I am sorry for what happened. If you need to talk to us, you talk to us, otherwise go back to your cushion and sulk. I defied the High Seat for you, and if that is not enough to see your value to me, then go ahead and fly off. And if you do, don't come back here either."

Shocked, Dime wondered if Volana would have let him leave. She hoped not. Yet, Uchitar hunched over the plate, almost shoving down the remaining bites of toast.

"Like I said, Dime, things are hard for lots of pyrsi. I will be back." Volana had barely made it through the curtain before she pushed off into the sky.

"You're staying here, right?" Dime looked over at Uchitar.

His head still down, he nodded.

A while later, wearing new, dusty purple robes and smelling like floral oils, Uchitar sat back at the counter as Volana served a broad bowl of spicy-looking noodles, dividing them between three plates. Sitting down, Uchitar grabbed a longfork and twisted at the dish, keeping his eyes focused downward.

After a while, Dime couldn't take the silence, well, at least the sound of noodles ascending. She wasn't going to pretend like they could discuss anything too trivial either, so she went to something that had been on her mind.

"Volana, what do you know of the Risers?"

Volana had left before Dime was followed by Intinpalo, who had claimed to be with the Risers and seemed to want Dime's help. Though, for what, she didn't exactly know, other than some vague goal to "reclaim" Sol's Reach. Rock said she knew more about them, but then she'd left in a tiff. Dime had meant to bring the Risers up with Volana in the Underground, but she'd been so distracted, the topic had slipped away.

"Bitter," Volana answered in between bites. "Set in their ways." She looked up. "I'm sorry, I shouldn't characterize them all so broadly, but that's the impression I have of the group. They want to take back Sol's Reach from the incompetent brutes, but they make no move to do so."

Dime didn't like that at all. "I mean, do you want them to?"

Volana's eyes flitted to the side. "Of course not. I meant that for a bunch of older pyrsi, well, they are, who have met for cycles to discuss taking over Sol's Reach, they don't really do anything about it. Whether I want them to or not. Instead, they sit around and rile pyrsi up based not even on facts."

She set down her longfork. "My problem is this. We are moving now, not just myself but the Foundry, to spread word that the solies are just pyrsi too, and that we should have conversations with them. But I can't just fight the layers of fear ingrained in all of us about the Great War, and the curse, and the metal weapons. Because of this group, I also have to fight the layers of fear the Risers have instilled. Stories about the Barrens really being ours, you know. A better place than here. Where we need to be. It irritates me." She picked up the longfork again and twirled up a long strand of noodles, slurping them into her mouth.

Dime glanced back at her own plate. For a pyr whose elegance and grace had seemed unquestionable, she sure was . . . direct in her eating habits.

"Where do they meet?"

Volana paused, chewing slowly. Then she smiled. "Yes. If you can talk to them, please do. I had been dreading approaching them myself. That would lift a burden."

Well, that settled it. The fact was, Dime had been ready to find out what was going on with Rock back in Sol's Reach. But she'd had an idea—a weird, probably horrible idea. But for some reason, her thoughts of the Risers' supremacy had reminded her of something: the pyr she knew with the least sense of it.

"Will you be alright here?" Dime watched Volana's reaction. The fe'pyr knew Dime would be leaving soon, but it still felt strange leaving her, knowing how unstable Uchitar could be, and what impact that had on her emotions.

"I will." She pointed at Uchitar. "We will distract ourselves by telling every pyr in the Heartland about the equally flawed solies."

Dime laughed. "Then I'll be on my way for now." She looked down at her plate of noodles. "I mean, after I finish these."

Intinpalo proved easy to find. As Volana had said, the Risers weren't much of a secret society. The place they met reminded Dime of a tavern, with plain benches and raucous conversation around long wooden tables. Yet, instead of the stone walls she'd expect in Lodon, with long panes of colorful glass, here the hall sat high in the trees, surrounded by rhythmically spaced vertical beams of wood. A roof slanted overhead, crossed by rough-hewn trusses, from which small flags and bells hung. Dime liked the way the breezes passed through the structure, and she almost sat down for a ferm.

Then she remembered she had short hair and no wings and was in a hall of pyrsi who spent their time knocking a culture they'd never met while glamorizing its home. That took the appeal down a notch, she admitted.

Heads turned and chatter exploded as she searched for

Intinpalo, calmly winding through the tables and peeking into side spaces. As she suspected, that meant he found her quickly, waving off pyrsi's questions as he walked Dime off to a private room up a slight ramp. Not quite with the pyrsonal accoutrements of an office, it was more like something a high-class pyr would reserve at a nice restaurant. She was almost disappointed when no one brought in a pair of goldferms.

She accepted his offer to sit, and swung a chair over to the table. She felt self-conscious as his wings spread, relaxed, behind him. One wing had a tear, she noticed, one that looked old, yet nothing could detract from the shimmery iridescence. As many times, now, as she'd been around those with wings, she always felt a little bare. She could only be who she was, she reminded herself.

"I have a proposal, and it expires now."

His brows rose. Dime couldn't help but note how different brows looked with hair on them. It was like they became part of the eyes instead of part of the face. But this wasn't the point. And Dime was not growing eyebrow hair.

"I'm going back to Sol's Reach. Flying chair." She gestured to the outside. "I'd like you to accompany me and stay with someone I know there while I run an errand. No funny business. Just a visit. Then you can come back here, and I won't tell anyone about it."

She threw up a hand as Intinpalo opened his mouth. "No. No more information than that. You agree or you don't." Dime didn't feel like playing. Not knowing that she'd delayed checking on Rock for this long.

"I was planning on resting soon," was all he said. "I've had a few."

Dime thought about this. Some rest would be good for her as well. Her attempted sleep had been ineffective at Volana's, as she'd kept an ear open for Uchitar. Then, a final sleep before returning. She wasn't going to bother Volana again. There were soft enough places in the forest to rest, and she'd done it before.

"Please meet me atop the Great Cliff in five spans. Just over where the primary entrance to the Seats' complex is. I'll wait at most a span. If you're not there, I'll leave."

Slowly, Intinpalo nodded. Without another word, he rose and left.

Interlude

It was the best party that Meilepa had ever seen.

Yet somehow, he felt invisible. Standing against the wall, he watched as friends and colleagues mingled all along the broad circular deck. He wasn't in Pito often, but when he'd heard all the architects were invited to the celebration, Meilepa had been thrilled.

Thrilled in theory. It was more difficult when he landed, pyrsi swirling all around. That's when the trouble gripped him. His chest tightened and his mind fluttered, and he backed up against the wall with wings spread wide, sort of hoping he could talk to the others but not really knowing how.

"Over here," his shiftmate called. She sat down within a circle of chairs and patted the one next to her. One step at a time, he walked over, instead selecting a chair a few seats away. There, he could talk to her nicely.

She stood up and flapped over to the seat just to his right.

That was fine. She was nice, and he'd enjoy her company here, next to him.

Meilepa couldn't handle it. He liked her; she was great to talk to. But she was sitting so close to him and there were other seats. She could have stayed on the other side and they could have had a lovely conversation. But she was sitting next to him and all he could think about was the lack of space between them.

Standing as if he needed to stretch, he moved over two seats.

"Are you ok?" she asked, peering suspiciously.

"Oh, yes, sorry," he said. He had to say something. She'd clearly seen him move. "I just have difficulty sitting right next to somebody," he stammered. "If it's ok, I'd prefer to sit here."

She looked offended. He'd offended her. Maybe he could explain another way. "You see—"

She'd left.

Meilepa rose. Now that he was in the middle of the space, he figured he'd walk to one of the cocktail trays. A server smiled at him, holding out a long platter. "Hello," he said, reaching for a small ferm in a beautiful etched glass.

He walked over to a tall table and set the drink down. Everyone was talking and having fun; Meilepa wanted to talk to someone too. Yet he didn't know most of the pyrsi, at least not well enough to simply walk up and join them. But there, there was the pyr from the arborists. They'd worked together fine.

He picked up the drink and wandered over, staying just outside the circle of talking friends. Yet he felt awkward here. No one seemed to have realized he joined. So, he walked back to the first table.

"Hi there," a voice called.

Meilepa turned to see his supervisor standing before him. Oh, that was nice. He reached to wave his fingers, but he moved too quickly, and his fingers brushed the glass. He watched in horror as the soft amber ferm spilled out over the white table and the little glass spun and rolled off, falling toward the floor.

He tried to stop it, but instead he knocked into the table itself, rattling it, just as the little glass shattered against the table's mosaic base. "Oh, I'm so sorry," he said, waving his arms futilely. "Is there a towel? I can help clean it." Pyrsi were looking his direction, talking to each other underneath raised hands. Unsure if his supervisor was still there and afraid to look, he scanned desperately for the server. The server had already seen what happened, but it had taken xem a moment to set down the tray and find a towel.

"I'll get it, Burge," the server droned.

"I'm sorry," he repeated, but the server was busy gathering the shards of glass. Another server landed behind him, giving the table a quick wipe before flying away. With a polite nod, the first pyr carried the folded towel back, presumably to the kitchen. Meilepa turned around, but the supervisor had gone.

Meilepa was alone again.

He stood a take or two, against the wall. The server seemed to be avoiding him now with the tray. And the music had started, and pyrsi were dancing, some on the deck, and others flapping their wings in fancy moves that carried them into the air and then down again.

Unsure where to go, Meilepa flew, himself. He flew up into an overlooking tree, one with a wide walkway that was empty for now. From there, he could see the party from a distance, watching the dancers flip and turn, and watching the pyrsi standing around the tall tables. He scooted back, letting his wings relax behind him and his feet swing from the deck.

Then, he saw a shimmer of wings. It was his shiftmate, flying with two drinks precariously balanced in her hands. "Here," she said, handing him one. Then, she moved down the deck, leaving space for a few pyrsi in between them. She lifted her feet up onto the planks, pulling her knees toward her with one hand as she balanced the glass of ferm in the other.

"Sorry about earlier," she said. "I thought maybe, well, it doesn't matter. To the party." She raised the glass in a toast. Being farther away now, they weren't close enough to clink glasses.

From where he sat, Meilepa raised his own glass. Pushing them forward, they both pretended they had clinked. He laughed.

"Thanks for coming up here." Thanks really wasn't enough, but he didn't know how else to say it. He was glad he didn't have to be alone.

"Sure," she said. "The view is nice."

Act 3

THE WEIGHT

Five bells later, at least by Dime's estimate, Intinpalo had still not arrived at their meeting place atop the cliff. She peered down the rocky plateau in either direction, hoping that even if he misjudged the location, she'd still spot him flying up and over the towering ledge.

Perhaps her plan was a mistake. Perhaps even a dangerous mistake. But she'd reached a certain point, bolstered by their ability to help Uchitar, where she couldn't become paralyzed thinking about all the webs she might create. She could only pull at threads within her reach. Witnessing the depth of Neimano's impunity as he even hindered their simple act of mercy had sickened her. She would not let fear of consequences dominate her own, heartfelt, actions.

A redworm poked up from a crack in the dry soil. She watched xem crawl away.

Her family was on her mind—Tum and Luja so far from here, and with the newts struggling over whether to justify the Violence against the Fo-ror. She worried for them, for all of them, and once she'd made sure Rock was safe, she'd need to allow herself to think about whether she could or even should intervene with the newts. And Dayn, she wished she knew what he was doing at the Underground, whether he'd found answers. They'd been so alarmed about the Boring Project and its threat to the Heartland, and she didn't even know whether the drilling had continued. Her hand ran across the ground, knowing Dayn was underneath it, though far from where she sat.

She hadn't heard the rumble of the drills when she was in the dead caves with Volana, but she didn't know if that meant they'd stopped. With the stream of new developments, she hadn't given enough attention to the Circles' drilling. But how was she supposed to keep up with all of it? She'd told the Light herself, urged her to investigate. From here, she saw no signs of the massive drills.

Seemed she didn't know much.

Dime leaned back against her arms. Though it was strange to admit it to herself, for she didn't feel comfortable around the harsh Intinpalo, she knew that he would be here. That he would not set her up or stand her up, even in the haze of awakening from what might seem an odd dream at the ferm hall. And that he would be here alone. Despite his misguided views, she could sense a code of ethics to him.

Which is why this plan had occurred to her in the first place.

A flapping of wings startled her, and she rose to her feet as Intinpalo landed beside her, kicking up a cloud of loose dirt.

"It's so dusty." He looked around, almost confused.

Dime laughed, though more from frustration than humor. He'd managed to visit her home for less than a full stride before remarking on it. "Dusty? Yes, it's pretty dry here. You get used to it. Just like you get used to that mud you were complaining about."

He scrunched his face. Now that she saw him in the light, not in the shaded light of the forest or the ferm hall, she saw his was a dark face, worn with cycles of life. She glanced back at the tear in his wing. Beautiful, really.

And being honest, she wasn't used to the mud of the Heartland herself, either. No wonder pyrsi carried a second set of shoes for inside. She wondered if he'd brought a set with him, or even if he had pockets large enough. As she'd noted before, his robes weren't made in the Fo-ror style she was used to. They were short enough to remind her of a tunic, and he still wore the sizable metal pendant.

She didn't see any reason to stand here and chat. "We're going into the city. It's a long flight; I must warn you. Also, I'm concerned about stability there, so if you're going with me, I'd like your promise you'll stay with me and not divert."

"I agree." He didn't meet Dime's eyes.

"Great. Understand that seeing a fairy could cause pyrsi great distress, especially now, so I'm not planning on giving you a tour. Just one stop, and you'll stay inside. Agreed?"

He didn't answer this time, but she saw no intent to deceive. "I'm going to use my chair to fly along with you. Understood?"

Intinpalo opened and closed his mouth a few times before finally speaking. "You're really one of us? I mean, you are?"

Dime grimaced. "That's a more complicated answer than I care to explain. But, sure, fairies did this to me. Not solies. Solies took me in and loved me. As you are about to see."

He clearly wasn't familiar with the term.

"Ja-lal. Call them solies. Or pyrsi. Not brutes. It's intensely rude, if you think about it."

Intinpalo didn't respond, and, at Dime's cue, they lifted off together into the bright sky. He raised his hand over his eyes as they moved.

"Not a lot of shade here for flying," Dime agreed. "Easier with my chair, but tougher on my eyes." Actually, she'd been thinking about getting a thin glass shield made. Maybe something with a dark tint that she could hook over her ears. She tried to imagine pyrsi's reaction to that, along with her bright white hair.

It was hard to talk over the wind, the distance between them, and the labored flapping of Intinpalo's aged wings, and so they remained silent as they moved on across Sol's Reach. Dime kept her pace slow, knowing she could move much faster than a flying being, and realizing that the fairy was much older. She hadn't thought through what a tremendous distance she was asking him to fly, but he did not complain.

As the daytime wore on, they stopped to rest and drink water from their flasks. She supposed they could have talked during these times, but they didn't, not until they landed just outside a ring of outgate villages.

"This will be our last rest," she said. "It's a lot like approaching Pito; the villages almost join together when you near the city."

"Lodon," he said.

"Yes." He'd said it sort of funny, but she noticed he knew its name. "Lodon," she repeated. Then, she reminded herself, the Risers talked about the Fo-ror reclaiming it, as they saw it, which made her feel heavy again. She tried to focus, especially with the city so close. "Well, we should be off." Again, they rose into the sky, Dime doubting her idea more by the stride.

Intinpalo's wings faltered as Lodon sprung into view. Once he recovered and was flying steadily again, she did smile at this, thinking again, as she had with Volana, what Lodon must look like in all its towering glory, seen for the first time. She felt certain, truly certain, that it was more impressive in reality than anything he had conceived or even seen in a drawing.

Though she could see the older pyr was exhausted, they were almost there. She motioned him upward and around, far from view of the wes gate and up to the nor. While what she was doing was bold, even by her recent standards, she didn't want to start a panic in the city by being seen in flight.

Having an idea and believing no one here would be sensing for valence, she dipped down and swept a mass of dirt and gravel into the air. Swirling it, she created a dusty cloud. While it might look strange from below, it would probably be hard to discern in the bright light and would block their distinctive shapes. If anything, pyrsi would see an odd dust storm.

Once they were close to the tower, she flew downward, dropping the gravel into a rock garden. Using the contour of the tower wall to keep them from view as much as possible, she guided the fairy directly onto the tiny garden patio where, as a ch'pyr, she'd sat in Sol's light and practiced her twist horn. Which, she'd learned Dayn had taken from their home and left here, in safety, along with other non-essential, but important items.

"Da-da," Dime whispered, sliding the patio door open. "Da-da. It's me. Are you here?"

"Squash Blossom?" Gorg's wide face beamed with joy, but Dime raised a finger in silence. "I have a guest. An unusual guest with views I'd like to challenge. Will you be alright? It might be a shock."

Gorg squinted; she supposed that had sounded pretty weird. By the time Intinpalo had managed to work through the undersized door into the modest living space, any trace of her father's uncertainty was gone.

"Welcome to my home," he said, fanning his fingers in a wide swath. Though he looked completely comfortable, Dime noticed his voice shook just slightly. Well, it wasn't the first awkward guest she'd brought home.

"Intinpalo, this is my father, Ma'Gorg. This is his home.

"Da-da, Ma'Intinpalo lives in the fairy city of Pito. He's involved with a . . . political group." Oh, Da-da was so smart. She could already tell he was on to her. "I have an errand in the city that I need to run. I thought, if you have time, Intinpalo could wait here until I'm done." She turned to Intinpalo and pointed at the floor. "You may use tree shoes here or not; either is equally polite."

Dime's mouth hung open a moment as she tried to consider what she could say to her father that would better clue him in without alerting Intinpalo.

Gorg just shook his head, like she'd spilled the grains and he was fine to sweep it up. "If you have business, you go on ahead. We'll have a great time." He turned to Intinpalo as if Dime were no longer there. "Here, take a chair. You must be worn out. I know here, in my mid-Dorh, I can hardly walk up the stairs without turning something funny."

"I'm new to my Eroh, and I have never flown so long at a time, not in all my turns."

Eroh! Dime hadn't realized he was that old. His skin was dark enough, but the way the dark twists of his hair framed it, she'd not thought through his likely age. Now that she saw how tired the pyr looked, she felt guilty for having taken him with such speed. But Rock had been on her mind, and—

"We'll be just fine . . . Blossom."

Dime realized he wasn't sure if he should use her name. She appreciated the discretion. And also took the hint.

As she stepped back onto the deck, her chair waiting in the middle, she questioned the wisdom of what she'd done. Would a pyr's mind really change in their Eroh? She knew pyrsi varied a great deal, but many Erohs she'd known had become set in their ways, perhaps as much by the construction of their mind as by the cycles they'd spent in it. And she'd been hoping her father wouldn't mind, but she didn't know for sure.

Her heart fluttered, hoping she hadn't just made a grave mistake. Yet, what would she do now, go back in and ask the exhausted fairy to fly back?

Taking a deep breath, she flew off into Lodon's sky. As she glided through the air, using the maze of structures when she could to stay out of view, she suddenly realized a great many things. That she had substantial hair. That Intinpalo, with long twists of black hair and wide, aged wings, had cast a striking image in her father's living space. And that her father had not taken a single stride to question how she'd entered in *through his deck*. After a sudden image of Intinpalo flying with Dime's stout figure in his arms, she could see why her father had presumed the fairy to be tired.

On top of that, he must have seen the flyer.

Uncertainty was not her friend. The pinpricks of anxiety over whether she'd done the right thing poked at her from the inside, and she forced herself to push them out, visualizing them disappearing away from her like tiny darts. She tried to breathe, hoping to ease the lingering pain.

Rock. Rock could distract her. She had to stay focused.

Volana had said Rock was rumored to be held in the city,

somewhere that would have a Sol's Pillars presence. Yet, it would be in private, from what she'd gathered, not out at the gates or in a public space. For all their flaws, the Circles would never condone anyone detaining a pyr, and so it would have to be somewhere out of view.

Perhaps the whispers had reached the ears of the IC; they almost certainly had. Yet as long as they were rumors, and not a thing that pyrsi had seen, the Circles would hope to ease them away. And without solid information on Rock's location, they would not search for her yet. Searching would only draw attention. If anything, they'd keep an ear out and ensure any hints be compiled and assessed, over time.

If it was true—if it was the Sol's Pillars behind this—Jaza would certainly know where Rock was. It was clear to her in their brief meeting that Jaza was not just a loud voice, but the pulse with which the Pillars were beating. The mobs in the city had been confused, disoriented. Jaza held ill in her eyes, and Dime had heard that she was an immensely powerful speaker, in her element.

Jaza would also have seen the posters of Dime by now. Jaza would believe them, believe that Dime could use valence. Then, the question was, if she knew her own history, did she use valence as well? Had she tried?

Dime worried, still, about being seen. She could deal with pyrsi here and there, but she could not cause a panic in the city. Trying to think this all through, she stopped in an empty rooftop garden. Chairs rested, overturned, on top of other chairs, with a backdrop of vine-woven trellises. A group of red flowers bloomed in a mound of treated soil, denied of anyone to admire them.

A smacking noise startled her and she spun around. Across the deck, a festival banner flapped furiously in the wind, its corner caught wedged into the rail. Dime stared at the lost banner. The object was so common during festival season, it almost wasn't of note. Often, they broke loose, or even were flown as kites or gliders between towers.

Walking over, she pulled it down with valence, and used a few pins from her pouch to affix the huge green banner across the bottom of her chair. She'd still try to stay out of view, but hopefully a flapping banner flying through the air wouldn't draw attention the way a pyr in a chair certainly would.

This still didn't tell her where Rock was.

Yet, how was she going to bop around town with white hair and a bannered chair?

Dime was going to rely on the fact that most pyrsi were good. Because if she didn't have that—

After studying her notes for a take, she flew to a ledge overlooking tavern row, just on the wes side of the market district. She wriggled onto an old staircase and walked past a couple of closed doors, down into a side room. The rattle and clink of table games clattered to a halt as she walked in, as did the conversation. This wasn't the sort of place for fancy dishes and fluted ferms, and as expected, the level of merriment was high. Pyrsi's eyes goggled at the sight of her.

"Hey, yep, it's me. I've heard rumors that a pyr is being held by Sol's Pillars against her will." That started a stir in the narrow, shadowy room. Anyone who might have been allied with the Pillars wasn't about to admit it here.

"I'm sure you think that's as right as I do. I'll find her if you can help me. Any ideas where I could look?"

After about the fourth tavern, Dime had a long list of places all over Lodon where there were rumors of Pillars' gatherings behind closed doors. Some she'd suspected had been to the places listed, and others had learned them as areas to avoid. As some of the information was shaky, she'd marked the ones suggested by more than one pyr.

Deciding this was as good a time as any to foster goodwill, she'd used the rest of Ella's remaining unmarked notes to pay off everyone's tabs. This was met with great cheers and wishes that she'd find her friend, and Dime felt comfortable enough she almost stopped and joined them.

But that had been taken from her too.

She'd been in the area too long for her comfort and knew she had to go. So, prompted by the ringing of bells throughout the city, she snuck back to the stairwell. Just as she was leaving, a pyr stopped her, sloshing out a huge mug. "You carry too much."

She stopped, unsure how to answer what seemed a pyrsonal remark. Noting the slur in the pyr's speech, she gave a polite smile and went to leave.

"I'm a medic," xe explained. "I see it in your eyes. Your expressions. You won't help the world rise if you are pulled down by its weight. Just something we say."

"Thanks," she murmured, unsure how else to respond. Making sure the pyr hadn't followed, she wound to the upper floor, found her chair, and took off again. Wanting to regroup a bit, but not near where she'd just been seen, she flew across to Nor Lodon, finding a secluded spot in the hills.

She hadn't been on this side of the city for so long that she'd almost forgotten how distinct Lodon's towers and spikes were from each different angle. She'd grown used to the imposing view from the sur, where the towers had a rich mountain backdrop, highlighting the reflection from their gold accents. Here, with the mountains behind her, the background was clean, clear sky, and the shining light of Sol. At this higher elevation, the towers seemed less tall than they did from other sides, but more striking, as the back section of towers blocked the view of the lower areas of the city.

She tried to take a moment to enjoy it, but thoughts and worries were buzzing in her mind, like drops of ink spoiling the lovely view. Frustrated and tired of dealing with them, she slowed her breathing and took each one and moved it away. Intinpalo with her father. Away. Rock, perhaps waiting. Away. The newts. Away. The well-being of her family and friends. Away. Even the Great War. It could not be her burden alone, or certainly not all of the time. Away.

The pain in her neck remained, and she pulled her shoulders down, carefully letting her neck fall forward. Slowly, she allowed it all to rise.

And finally allowing herself a place with no time, she heard the sounds around her. A creek, nearby. A bird. A rustling. Though it wasn't perfect, here at least with a clearer mind, she felt more empowered than she'd been in a great long time.

And she had work to do.

The bells again rang out over the city, and Dime had made no progress. With a sense now that the rumors were true, that Rock was in some capacity with the Pillars, the slipping by of each bell made her queasy and unsettled.

The locations she'd been given had been largely accurate, as either evidence of the Pillars' presence remained, or she was blocked by pyrsi who wouldn't speak to her or who even ran away. The way she was treated had changed dramatically since those terrible events outside the gates. Now, instead of shouting and following, pyrsi stared at her with fear or avoided her altogether.

The flyers, she remembered.

She thought of Ella, who had also reached a place where she could pass in the city, but only to silence and fear. And her heart wept. No wonder the pyr struggled with depression. Pyrsi needed other pyrsi to lift them up. Not to leave them in silence and alone.

Dime vowed to be the kind of friend who stayed.

Sol was setting across the city, and tired of the stress of the wild flapping sound under her, Dime rolled the banner back and placed it in the cabinet on the back of her chair. Her hand brushed against a pocket, and remembering, she removed the small carving of herself—the one Rock had made, unbeknownst to her, while they were resting on a ledge of the Great Cliff.

The Dime in the carving was serene and wistful, with a rounded slump and easy curves. She couldn't live up to the little carved Dime. Here Rock was, somewhere, maybe in danger, and Dime was no closer to finding her. With a final nod to wooden-Dime, she put the trinket back in her pocket, in the same compartment as the bag sheltering Ador's dice.

With a determined breath, she scanned the list. She remembered one of the conversations—a touchy one with someone who'd probably been a direct Pillars participant. Xe'd denied that the Pillars would ever do such a thing. The way xe'd said it, Dime got the feeling xe'd known that they did do it. Lies were the Violence, but he seemed to be justifying it to xemself.

And then another, equally defensive but even more openly hostile. What had he said? It was through the door, after he'd slammed it. "How incompetent does she think we are?" he'd said, met with a chorus of laughter.

But what did that mean?

She tried to put herself in the pyr's shoes. What had Dime done to imply incompetence? Only that they would have Rock, which she now believed? Or that Rock would be in a known location? Maybe that was it. Dime was searching places that were known, but Rock must be in a place unknown.

A place that was secret.

She couldn't imagine the Pillars taking Rock to Jaza's own home or base or whatever one would call it. Because someone would know where she lived. She was sure the IC did as well. Yet the way Rock had flaunted her disdain for the bold-eyed leader, it would certainly be pyrsonal for Jaza. And now that she was tipping off supporters one bell after another, Dime was running out of time. But, this was frustrating. How long had she been in the IC? She knew how to do this.

Calming herself, she took a clean sheet of paper and wrote down:

Need: To find Rock and/or Jaza

Know:

She tapped her pencil against the paper, opening up the map she'd made of the city. And she stared at all the known locations, remembering she needed to find a place she *didn't* know. She needed to tie one to the other. Then, how?

Staring at the map, it rattled her just how many pyrsi were involved with the organization now. Protocols would be hard to manage expanding so quickly. New supporters, a drain on resources . . .

This time, she couldn't be seen. Deciding to wait for night's cover, Dime sat, planning, as Sol set over the edge of the distant Heartland, far beyond her view. Carefully, she unlatched her diamond pendant. With an apology to the dice Ador had given her, she removed them from their soft bag, and placed her pendant in it instead. The dice, she wrapped into a tissue.

She picked up three large stones, weighing them in her hands. She wrapped each one in a sheet of paper, then nestled the diamond in among them. This whole package she tied into several more sheets of paper, using enough string to look properly concerned about its accidental discovery.

Dime flew down near one of the buildings she'd previously avoided, having been warned that it attracted some of the more fervent supporters. Edging along the wall, she took care to stay in its shadow, noting where the flow of the pyrsi seemed to concentrate. The doorway in her sight, she stepped nearby and spoke loudly.

"Is this the Pillars? Don't come around the hall." She spoke with authority.

"Yeah, but who's there?" Someone had moved near.

"I'm associated with the Circles," she said. "Have got something for Jaza. Don't need any publicity."

"Sure, slide it over."

"No. I want an officer."

The voice muttered, sounding uncertain, but then trailed off as the pyr left. Dime held flat against the wall, nervous even to breathe. She continued to glance around, making sure no one was entering this way. If someone were leaving, though, she might be caught by surprise. She hoped the pyr hurried.

As steps finally approached, she growled out, "Don't come around or I'll leave."

"You said you have something for Jaza?"

"Yes."

"Will . . . she know who this is from?"

"Yes. And I'm not interested in staying here and being seen. You agree to take it right now or I'm leaving."

"Please, Burge. We'll get it to her." There were a few voices now. "Your support is appreciated."

"It must be delivered immediately. And no one opens it except Jaza."

"Yes, Burge."

Dime reached around for someone to take the heavy package. Then she sprinted away and around the corner, where she got in her chair and flew up to the building's three-story roof.

There, she saw xem. A pyr had ducked out of one of the exits, her parcel in xyr hands. Xe glanced around. Quietly, Dime sat back in her chair and reached out around her with her valence. Yes, she could feel the energy she'd asked the diamond to emit. She felt it would last at least a bell, at least long enough for wherever the courier was headed.

This way, she didn't need to weave through the alleys and short-cuts, or care whether xe found a toothcar or stayed on foot.

She flew up into the dark sky, out of sight of the pyr, yet keeping her focus trained on the hidden stone.

The pyr continued on by foot, and it was a long journey. Impatiently, Dime trailed behind, distracting herself by watching the activity of the wes side, an area with which she was less familiar, but which had its own unique rhythm. Its pyrsi, carts, and toothcars flowed below, like whittleflecks spilled in water. At least the build-ings were shorter here, so she could fly above them and worry less about being seen.

She realized, after a while, that xe was heading for the Nor Gates, a series of pathways in and out of the high city and up into the foothills of the mountains where individual homes and retreats dotted the landscape, looking out over the towers and the plains beyond. After another check to make sure no one was following, xe passed through, leaving the city.

Eventually, xe approached a small building, low to the ground. Much less elaborate than others she'd seen in the area, it boasted no mini towers or dazzling sky decks. Instead, it sat in quiet anonymity, nestled back into the hills.

Dime wasn't sure what she expected. Would there be an entourage? A hidden hall? She was almost underwhelmed when the courier knocked on the door, and as it opened, xe bowed several times and then hastened to leave. Jaza stopped in the doorway, waiting after the Aoch had left, as if sniffing for something.

Then she looked down at the package.

Dime landed on the path and walked forward, hailing her with her arms. "Yes, hello. That's mine in there, but you're welcome to keep the rocks. As long as I can trade for the one in there."

With a flick of her hand, the package flew away from Jaza and burst open. Dime zipped the diamond back into her hands as she glided the stones onto the ground. She fastened her pendant back around her neck as she walked, slipping the soft bag into her valuables pouch, quickly returning the dice to their traveling home.

Jaza stood almost frozen, as if trying to decide what to do. "Well, she's been amusing me," she finally said.

If Jaza meant to sound impressive, she did not. Frightening, yes, Dime supposed that worked.

Dime strode past her, through the still-open door and into the home. She was unable to prevent a gasp, seeing Rock, right there, sitting against the wall with a bored look on her face.

"Hey, love. I hang out in prisons waiting for you."

Knowing Rock was often more intentional with her words than others realized, Dime glanced around the room. A small, black rope twirled around one of Rock's ankles, leading to a long coil behind her and then behind the heavy stove. Something about it bothered her, like an itch.

Furious and not waiting for answers, Dime threw her energy into the rope, telling it exactly what it was being used for. Jaza screamed as the rope burst out and slithered on the floor like a frightened snake. Rock leapt up as Dime spun on her heels.

"How the harm dare you commit the Violence against my friend?"

Jaza stood tall, her breath fast. "She's not harmed, you fool. She's the one harming our efforts. Don't blame me. Blame her. She wouldn't stay away from our business; she was confusing the ranks."

"The ranks? Why on Ada-ji do you want a war? Why don't you want to prevent it?"

"*They are the war.*" Her eyes blazed. "Maybe you were naïve before about what they did, but you seem clued in now. Who else? Who else now? Who in the future? You have children. Do you think they're safe out there, against valence and treachery and lies?"

"The only pyrsi I'm worried about is you and your Solharmed mobs!" No, that wasn't true. Neimano was dangerous, and Dime did worry that all of these distractions may be giving him the time they'd regret. She decided to ask.

"Have you met him? Neimano?"

Jaza hissed, her fingers spreading at her sides. "Do not mention him and do not believe him! Do not believe any lie that soulless pyr utters. Don't you see? Are you so stupid? He threatens all of us. You think he's done now? He's given up? He's decided we'll all just live together?" She threw her arms into the air.

"Do you think he dropped them off and then left? That was it, then we'd have a company party someday? *Why are so many of us dead?* Answer me that. Answer it!"

So she knew. Then how did she know about the dead? Had Neimano told her? Why didn't pyrsi just *communicate?* "If you know so much, why the kill aren't you out helping?"

Jaza stepped forward. "What the kill do you think I'm doing?

You're growing hair and, what? Floating around? I have an *army*. To defend us. To ensure that pyr does not take us over, or the Risers, or any of those terrible, disgusting beings. Don't give me your heroics. You didn't even figure it out until now? You're dumber than a rock!"

"Hey!" Rock protested.

Dime tried to catch up, but she couldn't just stand here while she sorted through it. Jaza's hatred was consuming the room. Thick. An obsession. She couldn't reason with her, and above all, she did not feel . . . safe. Jaza would not be the key to this. Dime looked at the pyr with sadness. "I'm not going to tell anyone, ok? I will take care of Neimano. We'll remove his power. Please. Stay away."

"I do not take orders from *them*. Including you."

"Jaza," Dime whispered. "Do you feel no connection? None at all? To the Fo-ror?"

"You want my connection?" she rasped.

Suddenly, a pressure built in Dime's neck, as though it was being pushed in. Behind her, Rock strained, also affected. No, she would not be tricked into this. She reached back for Rock's hand, grasping it, and with the other, she summoned a broom leaning by the entrance. It flew into her hand. Growing dizzier by the moment, she pushed the broom forward and it yanked her ahead, through the doorway, her feet lifting off the floor with the force of the jolt.

Both the broom and Rock's hand slipped from her grip, and they tumbled out onto the path. She sprinted toward her chair. Spinning around, she pulled Rock back into her lap and shot up into the air. "She can follow us," Dime breathed. "We'll need to distract her. Hold on; I can't stop yet."

Already in the foothills, Dime raced toward a treed hillside, keeping the chair awkwardly tipped back so that they wouldn't fall forward. Glancing side to side as her breath returned, she threw tree limbs and stones up and swirled them around, creating a storm of valence as wide as she could see in the darkness. She willed each object to fall slowly, giving any creatures nearby warning to flee.

Then, she doubled back, winding right back through where

they'd already been. As soon as Dime set the chair down, Rock hopped off and Dime stumbled to the ground after her. Dime pulled out her bag, wincing at the pain in her shoulder. "Sorry about that broom," she said, rubbing at the joint before she heaved the bag back up. "Was a little rough."

"I'm fine." Rock was scanning the area around them.

Pausing a moment, Dime removed the festival banner and crammed it into a side pocket. "We should walk a bit," she choked out. Noting the slope of the hill, she turned wes, away from the city. "Let's go. This way."

She swung around to Rock, remembering their last argument. "Do you agree?"

Rock nodded, and together they trudged off.

The foothills held no end of trees, shrubs, and outcrops, and finally, her legs about to collapse from under her, Dime sat back onto the dirt.

"We need a more normal relationship," Rock said.

"Sol, Rock."

"I know." Rock sprawled out against the ground.

Away now from imminent harm, Dime felt the weight of her guilt hit her all at once. "I'm so sorry I didn't arrive sooner. I didn't know what was going on. I didn't know if you were with them on purpose. I didn't know if it was even true. I'm sorry. I took forever to get here. Uchitar was in trouble and I had to sleep and, harm it I even—"

"D! I did not just spend all that time with Revengo just to have you whine at me about your *shit*. Besides, I was hoping it bought you time. She was so worried that I'd get away that it kept her back in that lair thingy. Not out firing up the campfires.

"That rope. She put chimney tar on it or something, to coat it.

But I knew what it was. It's that diamond dust, like . . . you know. I realized that when I couldn't use my picks to untie it. It wasn't really tied, it was more, stuck. That's how I knew. It was like Wayniam's key, stuck to her valence. Of course, it's me, so I mentioned it, seeing if I could get her to tell me what was really going on. Once she realized I knew, she wouldn't even leave the room. It was like she'd trapped us both.

"Honestly, after that, I didn't know what she'd do to me. Whether I'd be the first to go in her big war. If it came to that, I think I could have used my own strength again, like I would have tried using the rope. But I didn't know if that might prompt her to do worse, so I just kept alert, kept trying to see if I could talk some sense into her. Short version: I didn't. Anyway. She kept rezapping the ropes or whatever, just making sure I was secure.

"Not sure she realized how much that tipped me off that she doesn't trust her own valence. It's unstable or something. I think. I'll admit, I was starting to wonder how long I could take her blathering. I'd been playing through the options in my mind. Sol, D, she was so freaked out, she'd watch me *piss*. And then you just snapped the rope open." Rock chuckled. "Ah, her face."

Dime stared at the fe'pyr for a long stretch. She'd missed her so much. "Rock. I'm sorry for acting dismissively toward you. I didn't mean to, but I did. I value you as a friend and also as part of our coalition."

"Sol, you sure talk like sugar." Rock shook her head.

Besieged by a wave of confusing feelings and half-considering if she should just take the pyr back to the foothills, all Dime could do was laugh. She was glad to see Rock smile back.

"You have to stop flirting with me." The words just popped out, stopping the laughter on both sides.

Rock glanced downward. "I know. I'm sorry."

"At least, like ninety percent of it?"

"Ten percent's ok?" Rock turned up, but was looking away, like over Dime's shoulder.

"Yeah, sure." Dime just felt glad she was there.

There'd been no sign of Jaza, and they'd both rested a little. They each had a few bruises from Dime's broom toss, and Rock had been quick to show that hers were already smaller. "Holy soly," she'd added, enamored with the new term for Ja-lal.

Dime stared back in the direction they'd traveled. "I don't want to leave my chair."

"I know, but you could make a better chair." Rock sighed. "Look, ok Ella made it for you. That's sweet. But it was not Dayn-level craftspyrship. It was a crappy spare chair that she nailed a box on. Poorly. Ella would be the first to admit this. We'll make sure you get another one. And, besides, when things settle down, you can come back and find it. You'll end up the next Light and it'll be a collector's item."

Just as Dime tried to protest, Rock stretched with a loud groan. "Also, if you want me to stop flirting with you then we can't fly on it together anymore. Sorry. Rules of the road."

Dime laughed. She had a point. "Oh, wait until you hear this. One of the other victims started a fairy fan club."

"What?" This had Rock's interest.

"Yeah, fancy museum pyr. Was so excited to learn he was born Fo-ror, I had to talk him back from it. Like, whoa, maybe not all at once. I leave for a bit, come back, and find out— Honestly, I can't even say it."

"Say it," Rock ordered.

"The Fairy Fanatics."

Rock rolled back onto the ground.

"Do you know you are a Gamh?" Dime chided. "You know, right, that you're supposed to be dignified? And preparing to influence youth?"

"Please close your mouth."

Dime grimaced. "*Anyway.* The point is, if Dawn's Circle isn't working with them, maybe they should be. I bet the pyrsi drawn to Nafat's club have all sort of secrets." She remembered the thriving culture at the Underground, but she'd sworn not to mention it. Maybe one of these days, she and Rock would visit. Maybe, though, they wouldn't need to.

"Well, that's all great, since I can't be part of DC anymore."

"What?"

"You know, Atti didn't appreciate how long I was in the Heartland, though I didn't tell him that's where I'd gone, obviously. There was a note waiting when I got back, and he wanted me to grovel to him in front of his buddies and I wouldn't, and before he could fire me or order a hemsa or some killfft, I quit." Her mouth twisted. "But to be part of DC you have to be part of a Circle, because, well I can't get into it. So I sent *them* a note and that's that. As for the IC, it's fine, because what could they offer me?"

This was something Dime actually understood. "Honestly? Consider their betrayal complete. It's done. You're over it. And don't make the mistake I did; don't forget how many good pyrsi you worked with and how much love you had for them. Just . . . find something else you can do now. You're not over. Not at all. Perhaps . . . you're free."

An awkward silence ensued.

"Hey. New topic," Rock finally said, still looking up at the sky. "Your hair looks great."

"Really?" Dime ran her hand over it; she'd grown fond of it herself, but didn't know how others felt. Dayn said he liked it, but Dayn was . . . unyielding in his loyalty. He'd once complimented the color of a skin rash.

"Yeah. I can't grow it, though," Rock said, running her fingers over her aging, bald head. "Sorry. Too far."

"Be you," Dime responded.

Rock grinned. "So where are you going next?"

Dime cut her eyes to the side, not sure how Rock would react to this. "That Risers pyr? You said I was— Anyway." She was going to say that Rock said she'd been too open with him, but that probably would sound like a barb. "I took him to visit my Da-da."

As far as Dime knew, Rock hadn't met her father. But Dime had certainly described him, she thought. It was hard to say; that was so long ago.

Rock's impassive expression finally broke. "You took a fairy into Lodon. After all this, after oh no fairies went into Lodon, you took a pyr that thinks fairies are superior and should *run Lodon*, and you invited him to check out our digs, specifically your father's home."

Well, that did sound rather . . . strange when she put it like that. "Yes?"

"And I may accompany you to see how this is resolved?"

Dime sighed. "Of course."

As Dime and Rock approached the Nor Gates, Dime stopped in the last grove of scruffy trees. She sighed. "Oh, I forgot to mention. There are posters of me all over the city saying I have valence."

"Neat! So I guess we won't be strolling in, then." Rock tilted her head, thinking for a stride. "Guess we'll have to use that famous valence."

Dime glanced around. She didn't have her chair, or anything. "What's your idea?"

As Rock reminded her, she did have some nails and pins and rope. Without much effort, they pulled off a few dead branches and tied them together into a triangle shape, just sturdy enough to support Dime's weight.

Rock pulled an artstick out of her pocket and added a few more temporary tattoos across her forehead and around the top and back of her head.

Dime watched her finishing up. "I never appreciated how absolutely outlaw you were."

"I know," Rock agreed, putting the stick back. "Never claimed to be perfect, D."

She was pretty harmed close.

With Rock's reminder to stay hidden until she gave the signal, Dime curled up onto the triangular litter and Rock draped the festival banner over her. Dime used her valence and lifted the litter up at an angle, where Rock pretended to push it along, as though it had a barrow wheel under her. It took a few strides to get this rhythm right, especially in the dark, Rock grumbling some harsh words as the handles bumped against her legs.

Well, she should see how uncomfortable it was to be *on* it. Actually, they hadn't discussed what Rock was going to—

"Watcher' then! Shit wagon!" Rock called, as they moved toward the gate. Dime couldn't see what was going on outside the large banner, but she thought she heard the sound of pyrsi moving back around them. She couldn't let herself think about it, as she needed to keep the sticks off of the ground so it looked like Rock was wheeling her forward. And before the whole thing broke and Dime tumbled out onto the street, something she'd prefer to prevent. Especially now.

Rock whispered commands at her. A little right, a little left, turn around. Then finally, "Get out. Now."

Dime set herself back on the ground and jumped up, shaking off the banner, and stretching her aching back. Now intensely irritated with the swath of green fabric, but never knowing if it could come in handy again, she rolled it up and into her backpack.

She turned around to face Rock. "Did you call me a shit wagon? That didn't even make sense. Why would you be carting *shit* into the city?"

Instead of providing a reasonable answer, Rock decided it was time to burst into a crying laughter. She was doubled over, holding her sides, then she rose up. "Hey! Pyrsi got out of the way, didn't they? Enforcement pretended to be lacing a boot."

She started to argue but Rock waved her off. "No, not now. We've got to go. Ok, which way to Da-da?"

Dime glared.

In the dark, Dime wasn't as concerned with being spotted. Still having the charcoal blush powder in her bag, she did at least brush some into her hair, so it blended in more.

"You could do half and half, like white on this side and—" Rock stopped, seeing Dime's expression.

It was a long walk anyway, and they didn't want to pass too close to anyone. They went in sections, and ducked out of the way if anyone was going to pass by. Slowly, they wound across the city. As they neared Dime's childhood tower, she paused, staring incredulously at a ground-level park to its side. "Is that—"

"What? They are out in the open? Are you serious?"

Together, they walked into the park, and sure enough, Gorg and Intinpalo were relaxed back on a bench in the dark, each with what looked like a huge mug of ferm. Intinpalo's wings were spread wide behind him. "I know! He's so realistic!" Gorg was saying to a passerby, toasting to xem with the mug.

Next to him, Intinpalo was chuckling. The fairy took a long draft of what Dime was certain was Gorg's homebrew ferm. Brewed with fresh dropberries, the ferm was about as much a pride to Gorg as his folk tales. And by the dark hue . . . that might even be the good stuff.

Another couple stopped to stare at the ma'pyrsi on the bench, pointing and whispering at Intinpalo's hair. "What are they doing?" Dime whispered. Even if pyrsi thought it was fake hair, his head was still covered. One simply didn't cover xyr head in Lodon; she was surprised no one had called Enforcement. Dime ruffled her own crop, ignoring Rock's chortles.

"Oh, move along," Gorg said with a wave. "What're you going to drag down the Circles for two old ma'pyrsi having some fun? Now, have a nice night!"

Rock was snorting almost uncontrollably by the time they reached the bench.

"Blossom!" Gorg called.

Dime reached out her hand, and Gorg placed the mug into it. After a huge swig, she passed it to Rock. And yes, it was the good stuff.

"Exceptional," Rock muttered, lowering it. "I'll be back here for sure." She handed the mug back to Gorg. "Hallo! I've known your child here a long time. Name's Fe'Rock!"

She noted that Rock didn't bother to hide her name from the fairy.

Gorg rose from his seat. "Ma'Gorg; nice to meet you. Burge Rock, any friend of my child is a friend of mine." Rock smiled broadly. The two embraced.

Ok, come on.

Rock turned to Intinpalo. She paused, as if not sure of what to say.

Dime understood. She knew she should say something diplomatic, but it was unpleasant to talk to someone who thought you were inherently inferior. Trying to show her support of her friend to the older fairy, Dime moved closer to Rock.

"I suppose I see what you were trying to do," Intinpalo finally said. "I'll be on my way now. I—" The ma'pyr seemed to be lacking his words.

Gorg wasn't. Her father turned toward the fairy. "Safe travels. Hide and rest if you need to. And if you'd like to visit again, I suggest you reconsider your views. You've had a long life with a long list of influences. I understand that, believe me. But someturn you'll return to memory. Perhaps ask yourself, will you return as a ma'pyr of a stale, harmful past, or a ma'pyr that grew to understand and help mend? It really is your choice. Now, take care."

Seeming stunned by Gorg's direct words, Intinpalo looked at each of them in turn and then crouched down before flapping off into the night. A few passersby stopped, peering up, squinting past the bright light of a lamppost.

"What was that?" a ch'pyr asked.

"We're singing songs! Join us?" Gorg called.

Distracted, the passing pyrsi gathered around Gorg, who set his empty mug down next to where Intinpalo's rested.

Gorg broke into song.

> *All of my friends, gather around*
> *For the story of a wandering pyr about town*

He paused, and that's when Dime realized he was completely making this up.

> *The ma'pyr did not quite fit in*
> *The pyrsi stared and said who's him?*

Dime grimaced, unseen in the dark.

> *Yet when they sat and shared a mug*
> *They said he's just a normal . . . lug*

This wasn't going well, so Gorg reverted to one of his classics. Not just a classic, but a lullabye. One he used to sing to her.

> *You are beautiful*
> *You are strong*
> *You are special in your own ways*
> *So join me in this song*
>
> *We are beautiful*
> *We are strong*
> *We are different from each other*
> *Join in and sing along*
>
> *You are beautiful*
> *We are beautiful*
> *. . .*

Dime had always thought this a simplistic song. Yet the crowd continued to grow around her father's bench, with more pyrsi joining to sing the refrain and all the variations, and looking over, she saw Rock was singing too. And a tiny bit of the anxiety she'd been holding faded. Dime sunk into the relief; the pain had been more intense than she'd wanted to admit.

After a few more songs, pyrsi remembered they'd been out walking somewhere and started to disperse and, slowly, Dime, Rock, and Gorg picked up the empty mugs and walked up to Gorg's home.

"We have to go again," Dime said. "I'm sorry."

"You take care of what you need to, Diamond." He smiled warmly. "And don't feel bad about that; you never know how things might ripple. Now, how are my little ones?" Only then, did Dime realize he'd been worried about his family and she'd stuck him here with that pyr for bells. Feeling guilty, she reached out and held his arm.

"They're fine." To her knowledge, they were. "And I'm sorry I didn't tell you earlier." Suddenly, she realized Gorg would not shy from the truth. He'd rather know. "I can't tell you where Dayn is, but he is well. Tum and Luja? They left on their own." She took a breath. "They're staying with a group of newts, far from here. Within the borders of the Heartland."

In the extent to which Gorg's eyes lit up, Dime finally felt a moment of peace.

"Are they, now?"

"Yes. It's true." She almost told him it worried her, but she couldn't burden him further. "They're so capable, Da-da."

He almost looked annoyed. "Of course they are!" His eyes said everything else. "Do you need anything before you go? Food? Rest?"

"I could use the washroom," Rock said. "If that's alright. And a drink of water."

"Yes, this way. There's one in the floor lobby, with a pump."

"That works for me also," said Dime, feeling a wave of tiredness. It had been a long turn, and there was still one thing she'd decided to do. Now that she looked at him, Da-da looked tired too. "Da-da, why don't you go get some rest?"

"That ferm does make me sleepy. But, Sol, it's good," he added with a smile.

"It was nice of you to share it with Intinpalo," she said.

"Eh, maybe I was bragging." He winked.

Dime didn't believe that. She knew it was a message, and it was one she appreciated. Luckily, the lobby was empty, except for a pyr who'd fallen asleep in a padded chair, a copy of the *Caller* resting over xem like a small blanket. After a tight hug, her father started up the stairs, not looking back as he walked.

When they'd each used the washroom and were again outside, Dime turned to Rock.

Rock interrupted whatever she'd been about to say. "Your father is extraordinarily cooler than you."

"Yeah. I know. Anyway, I'm going to see the Light. Want to go?"

"Honestly? No."

Dime realized she had no idea where Rock lived, or even if she had a permanent place. "I don't know your situation, but if you need a place to stay, I can direct you."

Rock's eyes flitted to the side. "Yeah, I'll take you up on it. Long story."

"Sure." Dime jotted down the location and number. "This is my friends' place, Ma'Ador and Fe'Batu. They're spouses. They'll welcome you if you say that you're meeting me." While she felt uneasy offering up their home, she was certain they would want her to.

"Is Dayn there?"

Dime shook her head. "He's fine, but I really can't tell you now. I promise, I will when I can."

"You did also breeze over your children living with newts, but we can discuss that later."

"It's all been weird." She lifted her hands.

"Concur." Rock took the piece of paper. "Whelp. I'll see you back? And if you don't show up, raid the Light's Circle?"

"Yeah." Dime grinned. "Something like that. Hey." She reached forward, and Rock took the hug. Holding it a little longer than she'd intended, Dime stepped away. "See you soon."

Without a chair and not feeling like walking into a shop and causing a stir, Dime stayed off of the main streets and strolled up toward the complex. Really, she needed the time to think. She avoided the officers surrounding the front plaza and, taking a wide enough swath that she wouldn't be seen, walked around to the back. There were no entrances this way, except for maintenance tunnels and such, so no one else was there. While Dime already despised this method of flying based on her one previous attempt, this time she only had to move upward. It was just . . . simpler than figuring something else out.

Finding a sturdy branch, she gripped it with both hands, then flowed her valence, surging now with all of the extra use, into the stick, sending it into the air. Hanging on and forcing herself not to look down, she bolted upward, steering toward the back tower. It was an immensely tall tower, and Dime's hand started to sweat and shake against the stick. At least Rock had taken her bag. It was with tremendous relief that she approached the top, with its golden dome softly reflecting the skystones.

Yeah, Rock was right. No more stick flying, she resolved.

Sala's own room, while surrounded in windows, did not have its own deck. But she remembered a ceremonial one, just a few floors down. Flying to it and landing aside a group of very serious looking statues, she set down the stick and stepped in through the door, landing face-to-face with an officer, who, she presumed, was watching for just such an entrance.

"I request an audience with the Light." She hoped that Sala was in. She knew this suite included her living quarters as well, so she presumed she was often here, even if asleep or on a pyrsonal shift. To her surprise, the officer nodded and led her up the stairs, pulling a hanging cord as they approached. He stopped short of the entrance, extending a hand as though she should continue. With nothing to hide this time, she used her valence to open the door above her, thanked the officer, and then entered.

The room looked much different in the nighttime. Prettier, actually. While missing a lot of Lodon's glory, including the golden gleam of Sol off of the other high towers just below, in the dark it felt like reaching toward the edges of the sky. Dime was used to night views from the towers, the glitter of a thousand lamps twinkling, striped by gaps between buildings. Yet here, above any other tower, the soft light of the skystones radiated in all directions.

Dime could have stared for a bell, but that wasn't too practical in the midst of interrupting the Light. Yes, she'd considered that Sala could give her a direct order. Now, finally, she would be ready to disobey it.

A single lamp was lit on Sala's elaborate desk, where she had presumably been reading a book. The book was closed and set off to the side. Sala did not rise.

"How are you doing?" Dime asked, pulling over a chair that had not been offered.

Sala stared blankly back. Finally, she answered. "I talked to the CC about the Boring Project. I've been assured they are not boring to the sur. And if they were,"—well at least she didn't think Dime had been untruthful—"they are not now."

Dime wasn't sure what to say. But she wasn't going to get further with that here. Hopefully Sala was right.

Their leader slumped in her seat, almost as if weighed down by the dense tattoos of class and prestige covering her head. "I don't know what you expect me to do."

"I had hoped that you would listen," Dime said, her voice low. "I'm afraid things are worse now. I've seen the Violence break out in patches, as we've discussed. But more often, now. Pyrsi are justifying it as a need to protect themselves. But we won't need to protect ourselves if we ensure those who would harm us are not allowed power in the first place. Yes, there are pyrsi to fear in this world, as I've learned the hard way. But there are more of us than there are of them, enough to sway the path of peace. Only, though, only if we work together."

Without a response, she decided to just keep going. "I've been to the fairy lands. It's beautiful there. Flawed, but beautiful, just like here. There are voices, wanting to speak but unsure how to assist, when they are not connected to the structures of power."

Dime tried to meet Sala's eyes, but Sala was looking down. "You know Ador's heart. You know what he brings to this. You should leverage the power that he holds. I know they criticize the way you operate. And some will go too far. But the flow of ideas and feedback gives us so much power. That dialogue is like a rainstream, moving so we never stagnate.

"I also understand your hesitation. You know that the Fo-ror are powerful. They are a passionate pyrsi, and their energy has manifested into great ability. Ignoring that power does not protect us from it. May I show you?" Dime held out her hand, reaching toward a polished rose-glass ball, resting in a metalwork stand on the gilded desk. Sala nodded, and Dime lifted it slowly from the base using only her valence, turning the artpiece around in the lamplight. With all the finesse she could muster, Dime lowered it back into place.

She'd told Sala about Ja-lal valence too, but Dime still didn't understand it, and it wouldn't be hers to work through. Yet, there was something Sala needed to know. "This power, fairy valence, is being used by the Sol's Pillars now, too, by one embedded within. For the Violence. I have seen it, and I have been attacked."

Sala's head flipped up. Dime would not reveal Jaza's secret, but Sala did need to understand that, if her goal was simply to maintain peace through the status quo, that option was slipping away. With or without her.

"The Pillars are amassing what they view as an 'army,' to defeat the Fo-ror. We can't allow the Pillars to continue to grow, unchecked. Look, I know the Circles have sought to suppress their speech for cycles, and with this group, it's sympathetic. They are dangerous, and that danger should not be ignored. But restricting speech doesn't stop them from speaking, and it mutes the speech of those seeking progress. And to those willing to learn."

"Then what do you do?" There was no sarcasm in Sala's tone. She seemed tired. Sad.

"You don't prohibit speech. You don't frighten pyrsi who attempt it. You encourage dialogue. And you trust that, with education and transparency, pyrsi as a whole will disavow words of harm, will disallow them in their spaces, will take the air away from harm to breathe. And that, meanwhile, words of discourse and dialogue will thrive. And grow. And we will grow with them."

Dime let a small laugh. "I'm sorry. You're older than I am, and you've seen so much more. It's not that I'm trying to lecture you; it's that I've been through a lot lately. Isolated from everyone, in fear of how they'd treat me, I've had more time to think than I wanted to." The thoughts had plagued her really, burdening her every bell when she couldn't stay distracted. "Who knows if I'm right, but these are just things I've been thinking, through my perspective."

Sala finally stood and walked over to gaze out of the window. This turn, Dime noted, she wore flat shoes, not the raised ones she wore in public.

"All I've ever wanted was to prevent the Great War from returning," Sala said, lowering her arms. "The Fo-ror *are* powerful. They were powerful then." She turned back around to face Dime, agitated. "They would have won." She stopped, almost like the air had been taken from her. Then, suddenly, she no longer had the look of a confused or normal pyr. Before Dime stood the Light.

Acknowledging this, Dime stood to face her, fanning her fingers with a bow of her head.

"What are you going to do now?" Sala asked, though the question was spoken as a command. Dime had no desire for conflict with the fe'pyr, nor was she interested in being talked down to. She was just here trying to get her to listen. To think.

"We're already doing it," Dime answered. "We're forming a coalition on both sides of the cliff. Ador is the primary organizer for the Ja-lal, and an equally impressive pyr named Fe'Volana is organizing for the Fo-ror. They're in contact with each other. Without the power of either government in our hands, we are moving with urgency to spread ideas of compassion and goodwill. We are hoping, that when the tensions increase—and they will—that ours will be the voice pyrsi choose, no other. That we will all yearn for peace, and those who don't will have nowhere to find haven."

"If you're already doing it, why are you here?"

Dime felt as frustrated as Sala sounded. She'd supposed that was obvious. She hoped she could keep her voice respectful. "To find out if you're going to assist us, or whether you're going to get in our way." Actually, that'd come out a little direct.

Sala's eyes grew sharp. "Is that a threat?"

"Not from me." Dime almost laughed. The idea that she was the threat! That she'd spent these last turns just trying to make her way, and pyrsi were still pointing at her. "The Violence is threatening you, yes. Like it's threatening me. And everyone. Intolerance and ignorance and misinformation are threatening you. Me?" She shrugged. "I'm just doing my best. And hoping we can pull some harmstunk sense together so everyone can move forward with their lives. We shouldn't have to live in fear and separation. Any of us."

The silence between them was long, but Dime felt she'd said what she could.

Sala walked back behind her desk. "Dime, I'll think about what you said."

That's all I've ever asked. She bowed courteously, adding, "Light Sala, with your leave."

As Dime waved her arm to lift the doorway, Sala interrupted her.

"Wait."

Dime turned back.

"Wherever you're going, let me get you an escort and a car there. I'll make sure you aren't seen."

"Thank you. That would be nice."

Ador was not home when Dime arrived back. This was quite a disappointment, because she would have enjoyed telling him that she'd just arrived in an unmarked, privacy-shielded toothcar, surrounded by six Enforcement officers who'd said not a single word the whole time.

Yet, seeing Rock and Batu leaned back on the soft seats of the living area, she couldn't see making a fuss. "I'm back," she said, waving to them. Batu had told her never to bother knocking, and besides, this was the only home she had at the moment.

"Dime! So glad to see you. I've had a lovely time getting to know your friend," Batu added, starting to rise from her seat. Dime knew she was rushing to bring her tea or crackers, or perhaps water. Dime was fine for now. She'd get her own water in a minute. "I'm fine, Batu. Please."

Batu sat back again, though not before sipping from her own cup of tea. "You went to see the Light?"

Dime nodded. "I don't know if she listened or not." She glanced over at Rock. "It felt like not, though she said that she did. But you never know. So, anyway, I told her what we're doing."

"Really?" Rock looked surprised, but not upset.

"I did." Dime couldn't just go on the way she had been; maybe it was time to take a leap. Or a few. Time to move forward, to get to it. She almost said this to Rock, but really, nothing in that had changed. Life had detours. It always did. Small ones, sometimes. Sometimes large ones. With friends, friends like these, they could get past them. In fact, she had a new idea, one that had occurred to her on the drive back.

Truth was, she couldn't stop thinking about what Jaza had said—why *had* so many of the victims died? Kolk's condition was concerning. Cren had been forced to flee into the mountains, for reasons Dime didn't know. This left Olok, Nafat, Jaza, and Dime.

Sure, their troubles could be from the unused force of valence, of the subconscious stress of that power within them. But was that enough for half to be dead or harmed, only into their Gamh? What risk remained to the remaining half?

She couldn't let the idea drop. Yet, could she leave again, right when they were making progress? Was this about her or wasn't it? No, it wasn't so simple. Things were never so simple. Just as before, she gave herself permission to accept that each pyr contributed in their own way; the burden rested on no one alone. Nor should it.

Perhaps she was being naïve to let Neimano run unchecked. To not better understand if a threat existed. The agent in her would not be silenced, and finally she spoke up. "I need to find out more about the others like me," she said. "I'm sorry, I'll be away again. But I feel like things are in good hands with Volana and Ador leading them. And, I might not be the best pyr to have in front anyway." Perhaps it was the agent in her reawakening, but Dime's best progress had never been through being in front.

"We'll support whatever you need," Batu said. "We're here for each other. Always." Beside her, Rock nodded.

And suddenly, Dime was again feeling stubborn.

END OF PART 07

About the Author

E.D.E. Bell (she/e) was born in the year of the fire dragon during a Cleveland blizzard. After a youth in the mitten, an MSE in Electrical Engineering from the University of Michigan, three wonderful children, and nearly two decades in Northern Virginia and Southwest Ohio developing technical intelligence strategy, she now applies her magic to the creation of genre-bending fantasy fiction in Ferndale, Michigan, where she is proud to be part of the Detroit arts community. A passionate vegan and enthusiastic denier of gender rules, she feels strongly about issues related to human equality and animal compassion. She revels in garlic. She loves cats and trees. You can follow her adventures at edebell.com.

Continue Dime's story in . . .

Part 08: Leap

edebell.com/diamondsong